Mixing Business with Pleasure

Clint approached Alicia and cradled her two perfect hand-fuls of breasts in his palms. He squeezed them, popped the nipples with his thumbs while she sighed and dropped her head back. He leaned over to touch each nipple with the tip of his tongue. He licked them until they were distended, then took them and worried them between his teeth. She moaned and put her hands behind his head to hold him there—and then they heard the barrage of shots.

Clint jerked his head up and looked at her.

"Forget it," she said. "Probably some drunk cowboys. Let the law handle it."

"The problem is," he said, grabbing his shirt, "for the time being, I am the law."

As he put his shirt on, she saw light glint off the badge pinned to it.

"Oh," she said.

He pulled on his boots, grabbed his gun belt, and said, "If you're here when I get back, we can continue."

"Well, okay—"

But Clint was out the door.

THE GUNSMITH

382

STANDOFF IN SANTA FE

J. R. ROBERTS

JOVE BOOKS, NEW YORK

THE BERKLEY PUBLISHING GROUP
Published by the Penguin Group
Penguin Group (USA)
375 Hudson Street, New York, New York 10014, USA

USA | Canada | UK | Ireland | Australia | New Zealand | India | South Africa | China

Penguin Books Ltd., Registered Offices: 80 Strand, London WC2R 0RL, England
For more information about the Penguin Group, visit penguin.com.

STANDOFF IN SANTA FE

A Jove Book / published by arrangement with the author

Jove Books are published by The Berkley Publishing Group.
JOVE® is a registered trademark of Penguin Group (USA).
The "J" design is a trademark of Penguin Group (USA).

For information, address: The Berkley Publishing Group,
a division of Penguin Group (USA),
375 Hudson Street, New York, New York 10014.

ISBN: 978-0-515-15390-3

PUBLISHING HISTORY
Jove mass-market edition / October 2013

PRINTED IN THE UNITED STATES OF AMERICA

10 9 8 7 6 5 4 3 2 1

Cover illustration by Sergio Giovine.

ALWAYS LEARNING   **PEARSON**

ONE

Funerals were happening more and more often these days. As the West marched toward the 1890s and civilization, more and more of Clint Adams's friends, acquaintances, and enemies were dying. Some violently, with their boots on, others of more natural causes—in bed of old age, or of some incurable disease, as with Doc Holliday.

Clint rode into Santa Fe, New Mexico, to attend one such funeral. He left his horse at the livery after going over the animal's care with the hostler. The man was sufficiently impressed by Eclipse, Clint's Darley Arabian, that he agreed to everything just to have the horse in his stable.

After that, Clint went to a hotel and got himself a room. The funeral was to be held in the town's largest saloon and hotel, but he wanted to stay somewhere quiet. These kinds of funerals—and wakes—tended to get very noisy.

It was too early for the funeral, so Clint decided to get some of the formalities handled. One such formality was checking in with the local law. It was what you did when you were the Gunsmith and you were newly arrived in town.

He left his hotel and walked to the sheriff's office. He'd been to Santa Fe before, knew where the office was. At least, he hoped it was still there. Santa Fe was growing by leaps and bounds and may—in his absence—have gone to the Eastern police department style of law enforcement. He was pleased to find the sheriff's office right where he had left it on his last trip.

The shingle on the outside told him that the sheriff was not the same man. This time the sheriff was a man named J. Burle. He opened the door and entered.

The office was old style, with a potbellied stove, gun rack, desk against the wall rather than in the center of the room. Through another door he could see the cell block, which appeared to be empty.

He heard the sound of a broom and presently a man appeared in the doorway, sweeping dirt out of the cell block. He was tall, even though he was stooped to sweep. He was not wearing a gun or a hat, both of which were hanging on wall pegs.

"Oh," the man said, straightening, "didn't hear you come in." The lawman was either a young-looking forty, or was graying prematurely. Even his bushy mustache had some gray.

He set the broom aside, leaving the little mound of dirt on the floor.

"Sheriff Jim Burle," he said, turning to face Clint. "Can I help you?"

"I just got to town, Sheriff, thought I'd check in with you," Clint said. "I'm Clint Adams."

"Ah," Burle said. "Another one."

"Sorry? Another one?"

"All of you old-time gunnies are comin' to town for the funeral."

"Old-time gunnies?"

"I'm not as old as I look," Burle said, touching his head. "It's this gray hair. I'm thirty-two."

"Ah," Clint said with a nod. "What other 'old-time gunnies' are in town?"

"A few," Burle said. "Unlike you, they haven't seen fit to come and announce themselves. I saw Bass Reeves here yesterday. I think Bat Masterson also came in."

Both men were friends of Clint's. Reeves was a marshal in Judge Smith's court, must have gotten time off to come to this.

"Well," Clint said, "I guess I'll find out for myself who's here. I might as well leave you to your"—he gave the mound of dirt on the floor a pointed look—"work."

Clint turned and walked out of the office. He crossed the street and entered the first saloon he saw.

The funeral was to take place at Santa Fe's premier gambling hall and casino, the Crystal Queen. Clint just wanted a quiet beer, so he entered the little saloon called the Buckskin.

At the bar he ordered a beer, then turned with it in hand to observe the interior. No gambling, no girls—although it may simply have been too early—but the place looked like your basic whiskey-and-beer saloon.

There were only a few men in the place at that time of day, and none of them were "old-time gunnies." Clint realized that he and his colleagues were becoming somewhat anachronistic, but this was the first time he'd been called an "old-time" anything. It stung. Nobody wanted to be thought of as someone who was out of time.

"Here for the wake and funeral?" the bartender asked.

Clint turned and looked at the man. He was in his fifties, with a hard belly paunch and biceps. His hair was curly black, as were his eyebrows.

"How did you know?"

"Lots of people comin' in for it," the bartender said.

"People?" Clint asked. "Or old worn-out gunnies?"

The man laughed.

"You been talkin' to the sheriff," he said. "Man's got no respect for the Old West."

"You do?"

"Hell, yeah," he said. "We wouldn't be where we are if it wasn't for the Old West." The bartender stuck out his hand. "Kelly O'Day."

Clint took his hand, shook it, and said, "Clint Adams." O'Day stared at him and said, "Well, fuck me."

TWO

"This is a real pleasure," O'Day said. "Did you know the dearly departed?"

"I did," Clint said.

"Friend of yours?"

"I wouldn't exactly say a friend," Clint said. "We had a healthy respect for each other."

"Well, I hear there's quite a few of you fellas comin' in for this."

"Us fellas?"

"Legends," O'Day said. "Seems like we're gonna have a lot of legends in town this week."

"Legends" sounded a whole lot better than "old-time gunnies."

Clint put his mug on the bar and said, "How much do I owe you?"

"It's on the house," O'Day said. "Real pleasure to have you in my place."

"You own the Buckskin?"

"It ain't much, but it's home," O'Day said.

"I like it," Clint said. "I like a quiet place to drink."

"Well, when you get tired of the crowd at the wake, come on back," O'Day said.

"I'll do that."

Clint left the Buckskin and decided he might as well go and take a look at the Crystal Queen. Maybe he'd find his friend Bat Masterson there, most likely playing poker.

The Crystal Queen sat at the confluence of two streets, so that when Clint was walking, it loomed up before him. He could see several men sitting out in front, on the boardwalk, holding drinks as he approached.

As he mounted the boardwalk, he saw that the three men drinking there were young.

"Funeral ain't 'til later, friend," one of them said.

"That's okay," Clint said. "Thanks anyway."

One of the other men stepped in front of Clint, blocking his entry.

"Didn't you hear what my friend said?" he asked.

Clint poked the man in the breastbone with a stiffened forefinger. He knew from experience how much that hurt. It actually drove the young man back a couple steps, a look of confusion on his face.

"Get out of my way," Clint said.

"Hey!" the third man said. "What the—"

Clint turned and looked at the man, who fell silent and seemed to shrink back.

"You boys looking to test all the old-time gunnies who are coming to town?" Clint asked. "That's a good way to get yourself killed."

The man he'd poked was rubbing his breastbone as he stepped aside. Clint looked at the other two men to make sure they were stepping back, and then went through the batwing doors.

Saloons like the Crystal Queen were in full swing from the moment they opened their gates. This one was no different. There was music, gambling, and girls. A row of men stood at the bar, drinking. Clint looked around, didn't see a coffin anywhere. They must have had it in a back room.

There were several poker games going on, but he didn't see Bat Masterson sitting at any of those tables. Likewise, he didn't see Bass Reeves anywhere, but the deputy U.S. marshal was not a gambling man.

He decided to have a beer, since he'd had to run a three-man gauntlet to get into the place. He approached the bar, sized up the competition, then made a space for himself between two likely-looking cowboys who wouldn't mind.

"Beer," he told the bartender.

"Comin' up," the young bartender said.

The bar was long and there were two barkeeps working it. They both seemed to be working hard in order to keep up. Every so often a pretty girl came along with a tray to pick up a few drinks to deliver to the tables.

The bartender brought the beer and asked, "Here for the wake?"

"I am."

"You wanna start a tab?" the bartender asked. "Pay when you leave?"

"No," Clint said, "I'll pay as I go."

"Suit yourself."

"Where's the coffin?" Clint asked.

"We got a back room that's usually used for private poker games," the bartender said. "It's in there."

"Anybody back there?"

The man shrugged and said, "Maybe the undertaker. The body ain't ready for viewing yet."

"Okay, thanks."

The bartender nodded and moved on to serve another customer.

Clint wondered where his own funeral and wake would

be held, and who would attend. Would his friends outlive him so that they could attend, or would the likes of Wyatt Earp, Bat Masterson, and Luke Short die before he did? He hoped not, because that would be too many damned wakes for him to attend.

Too damned many.

THREE

Clint hit the streets of Santa Fe, wondering if he should make future plans for his own funeral. Maybe he should arrange for it to take place in San Francisco or New York. Or in Labyrinth, Texas. He could leave it up to his friend Rick Hartman from Labyrinth to see to it in his saloon, Rick's Place. He certainly wasn't going to have a wife or children to make the arrangements.

That was the case with this funeral. No wife or children to take care of it, so some of the victim's friends were putting it together.

Clint saw a familiar face going into a café across the street, and hurried over to see if he was right. Sure enough, Bass Reeves was just sitting down at a table. The big black deputy was hard to miss.

Clint went inside, waved away a waiter before he could ask him if he wanted a table, and crossed the room to Reeves's table.

"Any idea where I could get a good steak?" he asked.

"I don't know," Reeves said without looking up, "somebody told me about this place—" Then he did look up and stopped short. "Clint Adams!"

Reeves jumped to his feet and the two men shook hands.

"Damn good to see you," Reeves said. "Last time was when we had that chase in the Nations."

"That's right."

"Siddown," Reeves said. "I was just gonna order somethin' to eat."

Clint sat opposite the big lawman. The waiter came over and they each ordered a steak dinner.

"So," Reeves said, "passin' through or here for the funeral?"

"Funeral," Clint said, "wake, whatever you want to call it."

"Were you friends?"

"No," Clint said, "but I knew him."

"I knew him, too," Reeves said. "I'm here to make sure he's really dead."

"Like that, huh?"

"Yep," Reeves said, "like that."

Clint hoped Bass Reeves never had a look on his face like that when he spoke of the Gunsmith.

Over steaks they caught up on what they had each been doing since they'd last seen each other. It was pretty much the same. Clint had been wandering, Reeves had been hunting outlaws in the Indian Nations.

"Have you been over to the Crystal yet?" Clint asked.

"Not yet. Anybody there?"

"Not that I could see," Clint said, "and the coffin's in a back room. They said the body's not ready for viewing yet."

"Did you hear how he died?" Reeves asked.

"No, you?"

"No, just that he was dead."

"What'd Judge Smith say about you coming here?" Clint asked.

Reeves laughed and said, "He told me to be sure not to kill anybody."

"Well, that might be hard, with so many gunhands

around," Clint said. "I already met three youngsters who were on the prod. Got to be others, too."

"Yeah, I know," Reeves said. "With so many of us in town, there's bound to be temptation."

"I heard Masterson's here."

"If he is, I ain't seen 'im," Reeves said. "But I only got here last night."

"He's probably keepin' a low profile," Clint said.

"I wonder who else is comin'," Reeves said.

"Who knows?" Clint said. "Friend, enemies, looky-loos. The works."

"Should be some press here, as well."

"Oh, yeah," Clint said, "lots of reporters asking lots of questions."

"Lookin' for stories," Reeves said. "I could tell them a story or two."

"Guess I could, too."

Reeves pushed his plate away. He had demolished the steak, even though it had been overcooked.

Clint had eaten only half of his, but had finished all his vegetables.

Reeves pointed and said, "You gonna finish that?"

"Too well done."

"You mind?"

"Help yourself."

Reeves pulled Clint's plate over to him and started cutting into what was left of Clint's steak. He was a big man with a big man's appetite.

"Gonna have me some pie after this," he said.

"Sounds good to me," Clint said. He turned and waved at the waiter. "More coffee, please."

"Comin' up," the man said.

When the waiter came with the coffee, Reeves asked, "What kinda pies ya got?"

FOUR

They finished their food, topping it all off with pie and coffee, and left the café.

"Think the body's on display yet?" Reeves asked.

"I suppose we ought to take a look."

They crossed the street and walked toward the Crystal Queen.

They exchanged a few stories about the departed, and then Reeves asked, "When's the last time you saw him?"

"Hmm," Clint said, "I guess it was . . . four or five years ago."

"What happened then?"

"That's a long story, as I recollect it now," Clint admitted. "I'll have to tell it to you later."

"Hey, I'll wanna hear that," Reeves said.

"How much time did the Judge give you?"

"Just enough to pay my respects," Reeves said, then laughed. "He don't know I just wanna make sure the bastard is really dead."

They reached the front of the Crystal and once again there were several young men there. They spotted Clint right away, though, and word spread so that they stepped aside to let him and Reeves enter.

"What was that about?" Reeves asked.

"We've met before," was all Clint said.

If anything, the place was even more crowded than when Clint had been there last. But using Bass Reeves's bulk, they were able to find two places at the bar.

"When's the body go on display?" Reeves asked the bartender when he brought them two beers.

"Soon," the man said.

Clint sipped his beer, studied the room looking for friends or foes. He finally spotted Bat Masterson sitting at a poker table with a stack of chips in front of him.

"Bat's here," Clint said.

"Where?" Reeves asked.

"There, second poker table."

Reeves took a look.

"Seems to be doin' okay."

"Yeah," Clint said, "he tends to do that."

"Wanna say hello?"

"Not while he's playing," Clint said. "Best to wait until he's done."

"Your call. Think he's seen us?"

"Oh," Clint said, turning back to lean on the bar, "he's seen us."

Bat continued to play poker for an hour before pushing his chips in to cash out. He tipped his hat to the other players, and Clint knew he was thanking everyone for their contributions. It was the kind of thing that made other players want to shoot Bat Masterson sometimes.

Clint knew where Bat Masterson would be heading for next so he ordered a fresh beer and was waiting with it in his hand.

"Bless you," Bat said, accepting the beer and moving up between Reeves and Clint. He put the beer down on the bar and shook hands with both of them.

"Nice to see you boys," Bat said. "I was hopin' somebody I liked would show up."

"When did you get here?" Clint asked.

"Yesterday morning," Bat said. "I've had time for a few hands."

At that point a saloon employee came up to Bat and said, "Here's your money, Mr. Masterson." It took him a few moments to count out all the bills.

"Thank you very much, Leroy," Bat said. He gave the man a big tip, and tucked the rest away in his jacket pocket.

"A few hands?" Reeves asked.

"A few hands, but a lot of money," Bat said, picking up his beer again. "How about you boys? When did you all get into town?"

"Last night," Reeves said.

"Today," Clint said.

"Seen anybody else?"

Reeves shook his head and Clint said, "I've just seen Bass—and you."

"I was wonderin' if Wyatt was comin' in," Bat said. "They had a set-to a while back, you know."

"A lot of people did," Clint said. "I bet this town's going to be full of them."

"They shoulda had somebody at the town line collectin' hardware," Reeves said. "The air around here could be full of hot lead at any minute."

"You're right," Bat said, smiling. "It should be fun, at that."

The batwing doors opened at that point, and sometime lawman, sometime railroad detective Heck Thomas walked in. He spotted the three of them and came walking over.

"And the fun's just beginning," Clint agreed, wondering if any or all of them were on good terms with Heck Thomas.

FIVE

"Clint."

Thomas extended his hand and Clint shook it. He knew he was on good terms with Heck. They were friends.

"Bat." Heck shook Bat's hand. That left Reeves.

"Bass Reeves," Heck Thomas said to the big black lawman. "It's been a while."

"Hello, Heck."

The two big men stared at each other for a few moments, then they shook hands.

"I could use a drink," Heck said.

"Belly up to the bar, as they say," Bat said.

The room had suddenly grown quiet. Even the piano player had stopped banging on the keys.

Heck looked around. The four of them were now the center of attention.

"Go back to what you were doin'!" Heck shouted at the staring crowd.

After a moment of hesitation, men turned their heads away, the games started up again, and then lively, off-key piano music resumed in the background.

"Have a beer," Clint said, handing Heck a cold one. "Guess you're here for the same reason we all are."

Heck accepted the beer and said, "Looks like quite a wake."

"It will be," Reeves said. "So far all I've seen are lawmen or ex-lawmen. Some of the guest of honor's other compadres are gonna have to show up."

No sooner had Reeves spoken than the batwings opened and a man walked in. He stopped just inside the doors and looked around. When he saw the four men standing at the bar, he stared and then walked over.

"Am I gonna have any trouble with any of you badge toters because I'm here for a wake?" John Wesley Hardin asked.

"Not me," Clint said. "I'm not wearing a badge."

"Neither am I right now," Heck Thomas said.

"I'm just playin' cards while I wait for the wake," Bat said.

Hardin looked at Bass Reeves, whose badge was still on his chest. The two men stared at each other for a few moments.

"Far as I know," Reeves said, "Judge Smith ain't put a warrant out on you. That's all I care about."

"Well, all right," Hardin said, and moved down the bar. Several men got out of his way to allow him access to the bar. Hardin ordered whiskey.

"Talk about a situation," Reeves said. "When some other hothead gets here, there could be a problem."

"Hardin's okay," Clint said. "He won't go looking for trouble."

"Ain't he the one they say shot a man for snorin'?" Heck Thomas asked.

"That's not lookin' for trouble," Bat said. "That's just tryin' to get some sleep."

"I wonder if the local lawman will be smart enough to stay away," Reeves said.

"I talked to him," Clint said. "I don't think he'll come out of his office."

"Smart man," Heck said.

"Another drink?" Clint asked.

They all said yes.

"Oh, Lord," Reeves said about half an hour later.

"What's wrong?" Clint asked.

"The fella who just came in."

They all turned and looked. The man certainly looked like a hard case, wore his gun low on his hip, scanned the crowd with knowing eyes, and then approached the bar.

"Know 'im?" Heck asked.

"Jim Miller," Reeves said.

"Killin' Jim Miller," Clint said.

"If he sees Hardin . . ." Heck Thomas said.

"Or Bass's badge," Bat said.

"It's a wake, boys," Clint said. "Nobody's looking for trouble."

"Yeah," Reeves said, "but Jim Miller and Wes Hardin in the same saloon? Gotta be trouble."

"That's what some folks would say about us," Clint pointed out.

"We're not hotheaded gunhands," Bat said.

"We know that," Clint said, "but what do our reputations say?"

"Jeez," Heck said, "they're comin' in hot and heavy now."

The doors had swung in again and a well-dressed, diminutive-looking dude entered.

"Luke Short," Bat said. "Talk about hotheads."

"Didn't he gun down Jim Courtwright recently?" Heck asked.

"In Fort Worth," Clint said. "Yeah."

"Is he gonna be lookin' for trouble?" Reeves asked.

"No," Clint said, "he'll be lookin' for a poker game."

"You can say that again," Bat said.

Clint and Bat were both good friends with Luke Short, so when the man saw them, he came over with a grin on his face and his hand out.

"Good to see you, Luke," Clint said, shaking his hand. "Do you know Heck Thomas and Bass Reeves?"

"I've met Heck," Luke said with a nod, "heard of Bass Reeves. Nice to meet you." They shook hands.

"Have a drink," Clint said. "On me."

"Don't mind if I do."

Once he had a drink and a spot at the bar, Short asked, "Who else is in town?"

"Further down the bar from you, there's John Wesley Hardin and Jim Miller," Clint said.

"Together?" Short asked.

"Naw," Heck Thomas said, "they got a few cowboys between them."

"You run into them yahoos out on the boardwalk?" Heck asked.

"Young bucks with more piss than sense?" Luke asked. "Yeah, I convinced them to let me pass."

"Did you kill any of 'em?" Bat asked.

"They ain't dead," Short said, "but they'll remember me." He looked at Bat. "How's the poker?"

"Easy pickin's," Bat said. "Just don't sit where I sit."

"How would that change anything?" Short asked.

"Hey," Bat said, "you lost a pretty penny to me last time."

"Yeah, but I beat you the two times before that," Short said.

"Fine," Bat said, "let's call it even."

"When they gonna roll the body out?" Short asked.

"We been wonderin' that ourselves," Reeves said.

"Yeah," Clint said, "Bass just wants to make sure he's really dead."

"Same reason I'm here," Short said. "Just to look down at the sonofabitch in his coffin."

"What'd he do to you?" Bat asked.

"Beat me at poker," Short said.

"If you go to the wake of everybody who beats you at poker—" Bat started.

"Then I won't be going to yours," Luke finished, "will I?"

"Very funny."

Clint called the bartender over.

"Yes, sir?"

"Who's in charge of this wake?" he asked.

"Um," the bartender said, "I guess the owner."

"And who would that be?"

"That's Mr. Conlon, sir."

"Conlon?" Bat asked. "Ben Conlon?"

"Yes, sir," the bartender said. "That's him."

"You know him?" Reeves said.

"I do."

"Maybe you can get him to wheel that body out, then," Heck Thomas said.

"Nobody gets Ben Conlon to do anythin' before he's ready," Bat said, "but I'll tell you one thing."

"What?" Clint asked.

"If Ben Conlon is behind this," Bat said, "there's more goin' on here than just a wake."

SIX

The five friends continued to drink and talk, Bat filling them in a bit on Ben Conlon.

"He's a gambler, and well traveled," Bat said. "And I'm talking about overseas—Europe. The Orient. He's traveled and gambled and won. He owns a couple of places in San Francisco. I didn't know he had bought a place here in Santa Fe. I wonder where else he's got his grubby little fingers."

"Grubby?" Reeves asked.

"Just because he's well traveled doesn't make him a gentleman," Bat said. "The man's got no manners. I'm tellin' you, this wake is a front for somethin' else. He's got a reason for wantin' to get us all here—lawmen and outlaws."

"And in between," Clint said.

"Maybe somebody should talk to him about it," Reeves suggested.

"Or at least find out when the damn thing is gonna start," Heck said. "We might all be too drunk to gloat."

Bat looked at Clint.

"Don't look at me," he said, "I don't know him."

"You know everybody."

"Not this Conlon. You're the guy, Bat."

"You don't understand," Bat said. "I dislike this man intensely."

"Because of the way he dresses?" Luke asked.

"Because of the way he does business," Bat said. "There's nothing on the up-and-up with him, whether it's business or poker."

"I tell you what," Clint said. "I'll go with you to make sure you don't kill him."

"That'll work," Bat said. "Let's finish our drinks and then find out where he is."

It was unusual for a saloon owner's office to be upstairs. Most of them liked to be down on the main floor with their business. This was just another way Conlon was different.

As they went up the stairs, Clint said, "Maybe he likes to look down at his business."

"Whatever his reason is," Bat said, "I don't like it."

They walked to the door and Clint knocked. The door was opened by a man wearing a suit that looked as if it had been slept in. He had a massive head of hair that went in all directions. He was in his mid-forties, and his hair was starting to go gray from black, so it looked a bit salt-and-pepper at the moment.

"Well, as I live and breathe," he said, "Bat Masterson."

"Conlon."

"And who's this with you?"

"Meet my friend, Clint Adams."

"The Gunsmith," Conlon said. "I'm honored. Why don't you gents come on in?"

The man stepped back to allow Clint and Bat to enter. The inside looked like a whore's bad dream. Red and blues—red lamps, blue curtains—indicated that Conlon had little or no taste.

Standing in a corner, however, was a woman in a blue dress. She was tall, dark-haired, had a full bosom shown off by the low-cut neckline of her gown.

"Allow me to introduce you to Alicia Simmons," Conlon said. "Alicia, this is Clint Adams, and that is my old friend Bat Masterson."

"Your friend?" she said. "That's not the impression I get whenever you speak of him, Ben."

Conlon laughed.

"A pleasure, ma'am," Clint said.

"Indeed," Bat echoed.

"My pleasure, gentlemen," she said, inclining her head slightly.

"What brings you gents up here?" Conlon asked.

"The wake, Ben," Bat said. "When do you think it will start? We got folks down there gettin' antsy just bein' around each other."

"Oh?" Conlon asked. "Who-all is here?"

"Bass Reeves and Heck Thomas are standing at the bar together," Bat said. "And Luke Short."

"Wes Hardin and Jim Miller have come in separately," Clint added.

"Well," Conlon said, "that does sound like a volatile situation, but I'm afraid the wake will have to be put off until tomorrow."

"Why?" Bat asked.

Conlon spread his hands and said, "Unforeseen circumstances."

"Wouldn't it be a nice idea to let people know?" Clint asked.

"Speaking just from a business standpoint," Conlon said, "that kind of an announcement might cause people to leave, and it's very busy down there."

"Oh, I get it," Bat said. "This is simply a chance for you to make more money."

"It's all about money, Bat," Conlon said. "You know that."

"I know that about you, Ben," Bat said.

Conlon spread his hands and said, "I haven't changed, Bat."

"No," Bat said, "I can see that." He turned and left the room, leaving Clint with Conlon and the lady.

"I assure you," Conlon said, "there will be a wake tomorrow."

"Unless," Clint said, "there are some more unforeseen circumstances, huh?"

"Well . . ." Conlon said.

"Ma'am," Clint said. "Sorry we didn't have a chance to talk."

"Not as sorry as I am," she assured him.

Clint turned and left the room.

SEVEN

"Well," Alicia Simmons said, "Bat Masterson and the Gunsmith?"

"I told you they'd all be comin' in for this," Conlon said. "Did you hear what they said about John Wesley Hardin and Killin' Jim Miller?"

"I swear you get more excited about the killers than the lawmen," she said.

"Well, they are more exciting," he said, "because there is no telling what they will do."

"And what do you suppose the others are going to think of the wake being put off until tomorrow?"

"I don't know," he said, "and I don't care. I just want time to get more of them in here."

"Expecting anyone in particular?" she asked.

"Well, I wasn't expecting the Gunsmith," Conlon said, "so we're already ahead of the game. I was kind of hoping for Bat, which we got, and I'd like to see Wyatt Earp walk through those batwing doors."

"My goodness," she said, "you *are* aiming high."

"There's no point in living if you don't aim high," he told her. "Remember that."

"I remember everything you tell me, Ben," she said. "I'm learning a lot."

"Good," Conlon said. "Let's keep it that way."

"What do you think?" Clint asked, finding Bat waiting for him outside the door.

"I told you, he's plannin' somethin'," Bat said. "He's probably waitin' for some trouble to erupt, for the bullets to fly in his place, for maybe Wes Hardin to kill himself a Bat Masterson or a Gunsmith."

"Well, that's not going to happen," Clint said, "not with you watching my back and me watching yours."

"We'll have to warn Bass and Heck," Bat said, "that this is what Conlon's waiting for."

"What about Hardin and Miller?"

"You think they'd listen to us?" Bat asked.

"Well," Clint said, "Miller's bedbug crazy, but Hardin might."

"You're welcome to try."

"Thanks," Clint said. "I'll think about it. Let's go back downstairs."

EIGHT

Clint and Bat rejoined Bass Reeves, Heck Thomas, and Luke Short at the bar and told them the news.

"Anybody else come in while we were upstairs?" Clint asked.

"Heck thought he recognized somebody, but he said you'd know for sure," Reeves said.

"Where?" Clint asked.

"See the girl in the blue dress. She's got her hand on his shoulder."

Clint looked and saw a man he considered a friend.

"That's Elfego Baca," he said. "He's a hell of a lawman."

"Yeah," Bat said, "I've heard stories about him—from you, actually."

"He's a young legend," Clint said. "I'll go over and say hello."

"Tell him what's goin' on," Bat said. "We'll keep our eyes open for anyone else."

Clint took his beer with him to Baca's table. The younger man saw him coming and stood up with a big smile.

"Clint, *amigo*," he said, spreading his arms expansively. The two men embraced. "I assume we are here for the same reason?"

"To pay our respects," Clint said, "but I have to warn you, there are some large egos and crazy people in the room right now."

"I assume you are not referring to your friend Bat Masterson."

"Well, Bat's got an ego, but no, I'm not referring to him," Clint said.

"Fear not," Baca said, "I saw both John Wesley Hardin and Jim Miller when I walked in."

"Keep an eye on them, and on whoever else comes in," Clint said. "I think the point of this wake is to get us all together and hope that we clash."

"Lawmen and outlaws in the same space," Baca said. "Why should they clash, eh?"

"I just wanted to warn you."

"I appreciate that," Baca said.

"Come over and meet Bat, Luke, and Bass Reeves later," Clint said. "You know Heck Thomas, don't you?"

"I believe we met once before," Baca said. "I will certainly come and meet them. It's very good to see you, *amigo*."

"You, too," Clint said. He turned and walked back to the bar.

"You know what?" Heck Thomas said. "I think I'm gonna get out of here and get somethin' to eat. Anybody want to join me?"

"I'll come along," Bat said.

"Bass and I had steaks before we came in," Clint said. "I can't eat again until later."

"Speak for yerself," the big black lawman said. "I can always eat."

"Well, okay then," Clint said. "I'll hold down the fort here."

"I thought we were gonna watch each other's backs?" Bat asked.

"We are, but we're not joined at the hip," Clint said.

"Besides, Baca's here. Don't worry. Go and eat, and then come back. I'll keep track of the arrivals."

"All right, then," Bat said. He looked at Reeves. "You had a steak?"

"Yeah, but not a good one."

"Okay," Heck Thomas said, "we'll find someplace else."

The four men went out the batwing doors. Clint looked down the bar, noticed that John Wesley Hardin and Jim Miller were still maintaining a distance from each other.

Clint called the bartender over and said, "Another beer here."

"Comin' up."

Clint was halfway through his fresh beer and no one new had come through the doors. But he did notice someone coming toward him from out of the crowded saloon floor.

"Buy a girl a drink?" Alicia Simmons asked, sidling up next to him.

"What will you have? Champagne?"

"How did you guess?"

"You look like a lady who likes good champagne." He waved to the bartender, who nodded. In moments he was there with a glass of champagne for Alicia.

"Thank you," she said, either to Clint, the bartender, or both. "We didn't get a chance to talk before. I thought I'd remedy that by coming down here."

"What's on your mind?"

"I think you know," she said. "I think you knew it, like I did, as soon as you came into the room."

"Are we talking about the same thing?" he asked.

She licked some champagne off her bottom lip and said, "I think we are."

"What about Mr. Conlon?"

"We're business partners," she said.

"That's it?"

"That's it."

"Does he know that?"

"He should."

"Well, then, I only have one thing to say."

"What?"

"Lead the way."

NINE

Conlon came out of his office, moved to the rail, and looked down at the saloon floor. He watched as Bat Masterson, Bass Reeves, and Heck Thomas left, but he knew they'd be back.

Looking around the room, he located John Wesley Hardin, Killin' Jim Miller, and the young lawman, Elfego Baca. Things were really shaping up even better than he might have thought.

But there was more coming, much, much more.

Then he saw Alicia standing at the bar with Clint Adams, holding a glass of champagne, and he knew what champagne did to her.

He turned and went back into his office, suddenly not so happy . . .

Alicia took Clint's hand and with her other hand picked up the bottle of champagne. She led him through the saloon and up the stairs. They walked by the door to Conlon's office, passed a couple more doors before she opened one, and they went inside. She turned and came into his arms for a hungry kiss.

"I'm sorry," she said. "Champagne does something to me."

"Something good, if you ask me."

She danced away from him, found two glasses, filled them with champagne, and handed him one.

"Is it really this wake that brought you to Santa Fe?" she asked.

"What else could it be?" he asked, sipping the champagne.

She shrugged, drank some champagne, licked her lips. He put his glass down, stepped to her, and pulled her close. He tasted the champagne from her lips.

"Mmm," he said, "I like the champagne better that way."

"Then you'll love this," she said.

She stepped back, set her glass aside, reached behind her to undo something, and the dress fell to her waist. Her breasts were high and firm, like ripe peaches. She picked up her glass and poured the contents over her breasts. The champagne rolled down to her nipples. Where it dropped off.

"You're right," he said.

He stepped forward and stooped—but not much, because she was tall—to lick the champagne first from her nipples, and then the slopes of her breasts.

She cradled his head there as he lingered over her nipples, sucking and biting them. He reached for her dress and pulled it the rest of the way down so she could step out of it. Then she reached for his belt—first the gun belt, which he hung on her bedpost, and then the belt of his pants.

It was a comedy of errors as they tried to get his pants off over his boots, so he took the boots off first and tossed them aside. Finally, his pants were off and she was on her knees in front of him. She grabbed the bottle of champagne, poured some on his thickening penis, then began to lick it off avidly before taking him fully into her mouth and sucking him with abandon. She moaned as she sucked him, slid her hands around to clutch at his buttocks, digging her nails into his flesh. He knew there'd be marks left there when they were done.

He pulled his shirt off, then wrapped his hands in her hair as she continued to work on his cock with her mouth. She wet him thoroughly with her saliva, then washed him off with champagne, only to lick that off again. By the time she was done, his penis was red and raging.

He reached down to put his hands beneath her arms and lifted her up. He felt the slight stubble there, which he found excited him.

He kissed her and backed her up to the bed. When the backs of her thighs struck the mattress, she fell on it, with him on top of her.

He kissed her all over, her neck, her shoulders, her breasts, even under her arms, where he rubbed his face in that dark stubble. Even the smell of her armpits excited him.

Her breasts just filled his hands as he worked farther down her body with his mouth. By the time he nestled his face between her legs, he was reaching up to palm her breasts and use his thumbs on her nipples.

When he flicked his tongue out at her, she gasped and went as taut as a bow.

Conlon knew that Alicia had Clint Adams in her room with her. It was obvious what they were doing. She was curious about Adams, about what really brought him here, and wanted to find out, but he didn't think she had to sleep with him to do it.

He was angry, but had to control himself. After all, she was just a woman, and he had plenty of women working for him in the saloon. Any one of them would have been happy to come to his bed. Of course, the problem was none of them could hold a candle to Alicia. They didn't have her class, her looks—her body—or her intelligence.

So he poured himself a drink, sat behind his desk, and tried not to imagine what they were doing in her room down the hall.

TEN

Clint was half expecting gunmen to come bursting into the room at some point, but eventually he started to believe that Alicia had brought him to her room to do just what they were doing, and for no other reason.

Alicia had little in the way of inhibitions. She allowed Clint to do anything he wanted to her, and then came up with some interesting ideas of her own. Finally, she got him on his back and took his cock deep into her mouth. She sucked him avidly and wetly, bringing him to the brink of finishing, and then stopping. In the end she climbed on top of him, took him inside, and began to ride him. She was a burning cauldron, inside and out, easily the hottest woman he'd ever been with. As she reached her own zenith, her skin seemed to burn him, and his penis felt like it was in an oven—a wonderful, glorious, silk oven . . .

Later they lay side by side, both panting, trying to catch their breath. He reached out to make sure his gun was still within reach.

"Did you really think I brought you up here to have you killed?" she asked.

"The thought had crossed my mind."

She stood up and walked across the room, totally comfortable in her nudity. He watched the muscles beneath her buttocks bunch and release as she walked. When she reached the dresser, she opened it, came out with a bottle of whiskey and two glasses.

She brought them back to the bed and poured two glasses, handing him one.

"The champagne is all gone."

"This'll do," he said.

They drank and she poured another two fingers into each glass.

"What's your boss planning?" he asked.

"My boss?" she repeated. "I don't have a boss."

"Oh, right," he said. "Your partner. What's he got on his mind?"

"What he's always got on his mind—makin' money."

"Is that what you have on your mind?"

"Usually," she said. "At least it was until you walked into the place."

"That's very flattering."

"It's true," she said. "None of the local men stir me the way you do. Plus soon you'll be gone. It's perfect."

"That's not an attitude a lot of women have," he said. "Most women are looking for a man permanently."

"That's because they want to be taken care of," she said.

"Don't you want to be taken care of?"

She took hold of his penis and said, "In some ways—but not when it comes to money. I prefer to make my own money and pay my own way."

"Well," he said as she lowered her head into his lap, "you'll get no complaints from me."

Clint left Alicia's room after a few hours, weak in the legs and in need of a beer. He didn't know what had made his head spin more, her or the whiskey she was giving him. A beer usually settled him down.

He took a moment to look down at the saloon floor from the railing. It didn't look as if Heck Thomas, Luke Short, Bat Masterson, or Bass Reeves had returned yet.

While he was standing there, a door opened and Conlon stepped out. He joined Clint at the rail.

"Looks like you're doin' good business," Clint said.

"We usually do a good business."

"Oh, so then this wake isn't a way of bringing in more money?"

"I'm not a fool, Mr. Adams," Conlon said. "I know this wake will make me money, but I don't need it to save my place or anything. My business is quite secure."

"Then why not put the body out tonight?"

Conlon turned to face Clint.

"I know you think I'm holding the body back for some reason," he said, "but the fact is, the undertaker just doesn't have him ready yet. It's nothing I understand. But he assures me the body will be ready for viewing tomorrow."

"I see."

"Maybe you can pass that message on to your friends," Conlon said, "or anybody else who's curious."

"I'll do that," Clint said. "Thanks."

Conlon nodded. Clint walked past him to the stairs and descended to the saloon floor. He made his way through the crowd and found a place at the bar.

Right next to Killin' Jim Miller.

Miller had been drinking whiskey the whole time, and was quite drunk. Surprisingly, he was not belligerent at all.

"Ain't you Clint Adams?" he asked.

"That's right."

"Hey, lemme buy you a drink," Miller said. "What'll ya have?"

"A beer."

"Hey, bartender!" Miller snapped. "Bring my friend a beer."

"Right away, sir," the young bartender said.

"I got him trained," Miller said.

"I can see that."

The bartender brought the beer and hurried down the bar to serve someone else—or to get away from Jim Miller.

"So tell me," Miller said, "how well did you know the dearly departed?"

"Well enough, I guess," Clint said. "We met twenty years ago."

"So are you here like most of us, to make sure the bastard's really dead?"

"I'm here to pay my respects," Clint said. "Unlike most of the people here, I don't think I had any reasons to hate him, or want him dead."

"That's interestin'," Miller said. "So tell me, you think you coulda taken him? Face-to-face on the street? I mean, you're pretty fast."

"Let's just say I'm glad I never had to find out," Clint said.

"Yeah, well, I woulda liked to find out," Miller said. "I like to try myself against the best."

"Well," Clint said, "I think you'll pretty much have your pick here, Miller. Thanks for the beer."

"Anytime," Miller said.

Clint wondered how many of the others were like Miller. Were they here to try their luck?

ELEVEN

Clint moved away from Miller before the man could decide to try his luck right there and then. By doing so, he came face-to-face with John Wesley Hardin.

"Hello, Clint," Hardin said.

"Wes."

"What was on Miller's mind?"

Clint raised his mug and said, "He just wanted to buy me a drink."

"Yeah," Hardin said, "I think he's tryin' to decide which of us to try first."

"Is that what you're doin'?" I asked. "Looking to try your luck against someone?"

"Not necessarily," Hardin said. "But I wouldn't back away either. Where are your friends? Thomas? Reeves? And Bat Masterson?"

"They went to get something to eat."

"I see that Mexican kid, Elfego Baca, over there. Anybody else in town?"

"I haven't seen anybody else yet," Clint said. "Not so far anyway. But with the wake being put off—"

"What? Put off?"

"Yeah," I said, "the owner of this saloon is a guy named Conlon. He says the body isn't ready to be seen yet. At least, he claims that's what the undertaker told him."

"So when will it be ready?"

"Probably tomorrow."

Hardin shook his head. "There's lots of itchy trigger fingers around here, Clint. I wonder if we'll make it without somebody gettin' killed."

"I don't know, Wes," Clint said. "I guess we'll just have to wait and see."

"And speakin' of itchy trigger fingers . . ." Hardin said, looking toward the batwing doors.

"Clay Allison," Clint said.

"This should be interestin'," Hardin said. "You hear the story about him and Bat Masterson?"

"Never happened," Clint said.

"Is that a fact? Masterson didn't make Allison back down?" Hardin asked.

"No," Clint said, "and the story went that Earp and Bat Masterson made him back down. But I don't think anybody ever made Clay Allison back down, do you?"

"Probably not."

"Besides," Clint said, "I heard he's ranching and has a wife and child these days."

"I've known lots of men who tried to put down the gun and ranch, or farm," Hardin said. "It never works. And look at him. He's wearing his gun."

"Ranchers wear guns," Clint pointed out.

"Well," Hardin said, putting his empty mug on the bar, "I'm gonna get me a hotel room, if the wake isn't gonna be until tomorrow. See you then."

"Stay out of trouble," Clint said.

"I always try to stay out of trouble," Hardin said, "no matter what stories you've heard."

Hardin was referring to the story that had gone around that he'd shot a man in the next room because he was snoring. Clint had never believed it, but he didn't know Wes Hardin well enough to say for sure.

Hardin left the saloon as Allison presented himself at the bar for a beer. The number of guns in town was now at a dangerous level, with almost an equal number on both sides of the law.

Clint was at the bar when Bat Masterson returned. Clint waved to the bartender for another beer as his friend approached him.

"Here you go," Clint said, handing Bat the beer.

"Thanks."

"What happened to Bass and Heck?"

"Both went to their rooms," Masterson said.

"And Luke?"

"Found a poker game in another saloon."

"And not you?"

"I don't want to sit at a table with Luke," Bat said. "It would demoralize him."

Clint knew what good friends the two men were, and probably equals at the poker table. Certainly they were both better poker players than he was.

"I see Clay Allison has arrived," Bat said. "What happened to Miller and Hardin?"

"Went to find rooms."

"This town," Bat said, "and this saloon are powder kegs with all these guns here."

"And with the wake being put off until tomorrow," Clint said, "there's time for more to arrive."

"No wonder I haven't seen the local lawman on the street," Bat said. "I bet he's in hiding."

"Can't say I blame him," Clint said. "I'd hate to have to get between some of these guys."

"I'm thinkin' maybe you, me, Luke, Heck, and probably Bass should all be watchin' each other's backs while we're here."

"We can travel at least in twos," Clint agreed. "If Jim Miller keeps drinking, he's going to be looking for trouble."

"And he may find it from Hardin. Or Allison," Bat said.

"Somebody asked me about you and Allison," Clint said.

"Never happened," Bat said. "If it had, I can't see Allison backing down from anybody, so one of us wouldn't be here right now."

"That's what I thought."

"Speaking of Allison and Tombstone," Bat said, "I wonder if Wyatt will be comin'."

"Last I heard, he was in San Francisco, refereeing some big fights."

"I know," Bat said. "He's also been talkin' about maybe goin' to Alaska."

"Probably won't be here, then."

"That's not bad news," Bat said. "Kinda short-tempered since Tombstone."

"Who can blame him?"

"You gonna be stickin' around here?" Bat asked.

"Nothing else to do," Clint said. "I just finished the Twain book I was reading."

"I think I'll find a game," Bat said. "Watch my back, will you?"

"You got it," Clint said.

It didn't take long for Bat to find a chair, and then he was engrossed in a draw poker game. Clint ordered another beer and settled down to keep an eye on his friend's back.

TWELVE

Before long, Bat Masterson had a stack of chips in front of him. Clint could see that it had also come to the attention of some other men in the place. He didn't recognize them as anyone who might be there for the wake. He thought they were just there looking for trouble.

They were young, in their late twenties, and had been drinking a lot. Now they were nudging each other and pointing over toward the table Masterson was at.

Clint grabbed a saloon girl who was going by at that moment.

"Excuse me, what's your name?"

The woman was young, blond, and pretty.

"My name's Karen. What can I do for you, handsome?" she asked, blinking her big blue eyes at him.

"I'd like you to take three beers over to that table," he said, pointing.

"You're buyin' them a drink?"

"Do you know them?"

"I do," she said. "They can get good and drunk all on their own, believe me."

"Well, bring them the beers anyway."

"Do you want me to tell them the drinks are from you?"

"No," he said, "I'll take care of that myself."

"Well, okay."

She went to the bartender, got three mugs of beer, and brought them over to the three young men. Two of them tried to grope her, but she avoided them as if she'd had great practice doing it.

She walked by Clint and said, "There ya go."

He put some money on her tray and said, "Thank you, Karen."

She shrugged and moved on.

Clint picked up his own beer and went to join the three men.

"Mind if I sit down?" he asked, then sat without waiting for an answer.

"What do you want, mister?" one of them asked.

"You're crashing a private party, friend," another one said.

"Really?" Clint asked. "I thought seeing as how I supplied the drinks, maybe I was invited."

"You bought the beers?" the third man asked.

"That's right," Clint said. "You mind if I ask, are you boys from town?"

"That's right," the first one said.

"We work around here," the second one said. "So?"

"What are your names?"

None of them answered.

"Hey," he said, "you're drinking my beer, I should at least know your names."

"Sam," the first one said.

"Ted," the second man said.

"My name's Al," the third said. "So what's your name, mister?"

"My name's Clint Adams."

The three men stared at him.

"The Gunsmith?" Sam asked.

"That's right."

"W-What are you doin' here?" Ted asked. "With us?"

"Well," Clint said, "I noticed the three of you looking over at my friend, at that poker table."

"Your friend?"

"Yes," Clint said, "the one with all the chips in front of him? I had the feeling you were getting the wrong idea."

"What idea?" Al asked.

"Like maybe trying to relieve him of his money?"

The three young men exchanged glances nervously.

"You should all know," Clint said, "who that is you're thinking about robbing."

"Whataya mean?" Sam asked. "He's a tinhorn gambler."

"A tinhorn gambler named Bat Masterson," Clint said.

Their eyes widened.

"Yes. If you had been foolish enough to try to rob him, you would have ended up dead," Clint told them. "So drink up and be happy I came over to warn you."

They all picked up their beers and drank.

THIRTEEN

Clint returned to the bar with the rest of his beer.

"You saved their lives," someone said.

He turned his head and looked. Standing next to him was Bill Tilghman, the former marshal of Dodge City, but now a rancher.

"Hello, Bill."

"Thought I was sneakin up on you," Tilghman said.

"No, I saw you."

"Still aware, eh?"

"I haven't lost my senses yet," Clint said. "I'm not that old."

Tilghman, older than Clint and sporting some gray in his bushy mustache, said, "With age comes great wisdom."

"Then I admit," Clint said, "that you are the wiser of the two of us."

"That means you're buyin'."

Clint signaled to the bartender to give Tilghman a beer. Clint was still working on his own. He'd consumed quite a few by now. He was trying to slow down.

"When did you get to town?" Clint asked.

"About two hours ago. Stopped for somethin' to eat before comin' here. When's the wake?"

"Tomorrow."

"I thought it was today."

"It was supposed to be," Clint said. "Change of plans."

"By who?"

"Fella who owns the joint," Clint said. "His name's Conlon. Know him?"

"I know of a Ben Conlon."

"That's him."

"Then there's money to be made," Tilghman said, "or he wouldn't be here."

"Look around," Clint said. "He's makin' plenty of money."

"I mean from the wake," Tilghman said. "Is he charging admission?"

"No."

"Then he's up to somethin'."

"More than what you see here?"

"Seems like it," Tilghman said. "I saw Allison when I came in, Bat playing poker, Jim Miller later. On the street I spotted Wes Hardin."

"And more," Clint said. "Bass Reeves, Heck Thomas, and Luke Short."

"Trouble, trouble, and trouble," Tilghman said.

"And why are you here?"

"Not for trouble," Tilghman said. "Just to pay my respects."

"That's why I'm here," Clint said, "but most of the men here just want to make sure he's dead."

"Well," Tilghman said, "I can't blame them for that. You or I may not have had anythin' against him, but others certainly do."

Clint finished his beer, contemplated another. It was at his elbow before he could decide, with Bill Tilghman paying.

"Thanks."

"What was your business with those three?" Tilghman said, jerking his chin toward the table where Sam, Ted, and Al sat.

"Like you said," Clint replied, "I saved their lives."

"So they were eyeing Bat's chips, eh?"

"They were."

"And why aren't you playin'?"

"Because I might end up in a game with Bat or Luke," Clint said.

"You can handle them," Tilghman said. "I've seen you play."

"I'm on a bad streak," Clint said. "The cards haven't been coming to me lately. That's not a time to try to tangle with men whose skills transcend the cards."

"Meaning?"

"They don't need good cards in order to win," Clint said. "I do."

"You're modest," Tilghman said, "but I wouldn't want to play against them either." Tilghman smiled. "Maybe you just don't want to take money from friends."

"That could be it, too."

Tilghman looked around. "Well, there are enough pretty girls here to keep you occupied."

"And one lovely woman," Clint said, looking up at the second floor.

Tilghman looked also and saw Alicia Simmons staring down from the balcony.

"Oh," he said, "I see."

FOURTEEN

The drinking and music and poker went on into the night, and on to morning. Conlon had decided to stay open as long as he could, until the law closed him down. Yet the law never appeared.

Conlon himself decided enough was enough around 6 a.m.

Clint stuck it out all night, as did Bat. The others faded away a few at a time.

"Closing time," the bartender called.

The poker game broke up, and Bat joined Clint at the bar, where there was now plenty of room.

"The sheriff never showed up to close the place down," Bat observed. "Still playin' it smart, I guess."

They had coffee before they left, found they were staying in the same hotel, the Chatwith House.

"Best in town," Bat said. "Undoubtedly, Luke is also here."

"No doubt," Clint agreed.

"Breakfast?" Bat asked.

"Now or later?" Clint asked.

"Well, now," Bat said. "Later it would be lunch."

"Breakfast, it is."

* * *

They got a table in the hotel dining room, which had just opened to serve breakfast.

"None of our colleagues are up yet," Bat said, looking around. "I saw Tilghman standin' with you for a while."

"Yeah, he had only just arrived a couple of hours before," Clint said.

"I wonder who will arrive today," Bat said. "A whole day for more guns to arrive. If this town doesn't explode, I'll be shocked."

Clint and Bat both ordered steak and eggs, and coffee.

"Lots and lots of strong coffee," Bat said.

"You plan on staying up?" Clint asked.

"Possibly. I'm just not sleepy."

"Odd," Clint said, "but neither am I."

"You see?" Bat asked. "We're both feelin' the same thing. Somethin's gonna happen that we don't want to miss."

"Or maybe we can stop."

"I also saw you talk to those three whelps who were thinkin' about robbin' me."

"They were drunk and stupid," Clint said. "I saved their lives."

"Oh, I wouldn't have killed them," Bat said. "At least, I don't think so."

The waiter brought the coffee, poured it for them.

"Maybe we should talk with the sheriff," Bat said. "See how many deputies he has."

"Are you thinking of volunteering?"

"Me? No. Maybe you, though."

"Not me," Clint said. "Burle must have his own deputies."

"You've met the sheriff?"

"I have," Clint said. "Stopped in to see him upon my arrival. He was . . . unimpressive, but I don't know yet if he's smart or cowardly."

"Smart to stay out of the saloon, I'd say," Bat said. "Why look for trouble?"

"To keep it from happening."

"Spoken like a true ex-lawman," Bat said, "but we do have lawmen in town. Bass Reeves still wears a badge. What about Tilghman?"

"Not for a while," Clint said. "Ranching."

"But more recently than we have," Bat said. "He'll still hold that mind-set."

"Maybe."

"Well," Bat said as the waiter arrived with their plates, "we have other matters to attend to now."

Clint looked down at the plate laden with steak and eggs and said, "So we do."

FIFTEEN

After breakfast Clint and Bat stepped outside the hotel and watched as the town awoke. People on the streets, wagons and buckboards carrying people and supplies.

"Looks peaceful enough," Bat said.

"Well," Clint said, "everyone but us is asleep. Wait until they wake up and hit the streets."

"The trouble will most likely come from Miller, Hardin, or Allison," Bat said.

"That's what I figure," Clint said, "or from some local who's feeling brave and stupid."

"Who else is there to arrive but Wyatt, Virgil . . ."

"What about James?"

"My brother won't be here."

"Then there's Siringo, and Tom Horn . . . I ran across them both sometime back. Working together."

"That must have been an experience."

"Speaking of lawmen," Clint said, "we forgot Baca. He still wears a badge."

"Then the sheriff should have all the help he needs, and not expect any from us."

"Agreed."

"I think I'm gonna to see if the general store is open yet," Bat said. "I need some good cigars."

"I think," Clint said, "I'm going to pull up one of these chairs and just sit awhile. I'll be here in case you run into any trouble."

"If I do," Bat said, "you'll be the first to know."

Bat stepped into the street and crossed while Clint sat in a wooden chair and leaned it back against the wall.

While Clint was sitting in front of the hotel and relaxing, more and more people appeared on the streets. Some of them nodded to him when they passed; some women even graced him with smiles. More and more buckboards rolled by as businesses got rolling. And then a man on a black horse rode down the center of the street. Clint recognized him immediately, and knew that trouble had definitely come to town.

Dutch Craddock was a bounty hunter, and whether his prey was worth money alive or dead, he brought them back dead.

Every time.

Craddock spotted Clint Adams as soon as he came within sight of the hotel. He directed his horse that way, stopped right in front of the seated Gunsmith.

"Adams."

"Dutch," Clint said. "Here for the wake?"

"What wake?"

"You haven't heard?"

"I'm not here for any wake, Adams," Craddock said, "unless the man I'm lookin' for makes me kill 'im."

"Don't they all make you kill them, Dutch?"

"Hey," Dutch said, "the paper says dead or alive. I leave the choice up to them."

"Seems to me they always make the wrong choice."

"So you're here for some wake?" Craddock asked.

"I'm here for the wake. It's—"

"I don't even want to know," Craddock said. "It doesn't matter to me. You stayin' in this hotel?"

"I am."

"Any good?"

"The best one in town."

"They still got rooms?"

"There are a lot of people in town for the wake, but I think they do."

"Good," Craddock said. "I'll see to my horse first."

Craddock started to wheel his horse around when Clint called out, "You didn't say who you were here looking for."

"No," Craddock said, "I didn't."

He rode away.

Bat returned smoking a big cigar but looking a bit sleepy.

"You still sittin' here?" he asked. "I thought you'd be in bed by now." He pulled a chair over and sat next to Clint. "What's been goin' on?"

"Another gun came to town."

"Oh? Who was it this time?"

"Dutch Craddock."

"Craddock?" Bat asked, pausing with the cigar almost to his mouth. "What's he here for?"

"Not what," Clint said. "Who? He doesn't know anything about the wake. Didn't even want to know who the wake was for. Just if this was a good hotel."

"Well, if he's not here for the wake, who's he here for?" Bat asked.

"He didn't say."

Bat put the cigar in his mouth and twirled it while he thought.

"It's got to be somebody with a price on his head," he said. "That leaves out you, me, Luke, Heck, Bass, and Elfego Baca."

"Right," Clint said, "but that leaves in Hardin, Allison, and Jim Miller."

"Unless it's somebody else," Bat said, "and Craddock got here first."

"The question is," Clint said, "will he be tempted to go against one of them while he's waiting?"

"I haven't heard that Craddock ever had anything to prove," Bat said. "He's fast, I know that . . ."

"But he doesn't need to prove it," Clint said.

"Then why does he bring in all his bounties dead?"

"I guess it's just easier for him that way," Clint said.

"I wonder what the local sheriff will think about Craddock being in town."

"If I remember correctly," Clint said, "Craddock usually checks in with the locals, so I guess we'll find out."

"You know what?" Bat asked.

"What?"

Bat looked at the tip of his cigar and said, "I'm gonna finish this cigar and then get some sleep."

"I think," Clint said, letting the front legs of his chair come down, "I'll have a talk with the sheriff."

"Gonna check him out for real this time?" Bat asked. "See what he's made of?"

"Might as well find out if he's going to do his job or not," Clint said.

"Well," Bat said, "let me know what you decide—when I wake up."

"I'll do that," Clint said. "Sleep well."

SIXTEEN

Sheriff Jim Burle looked up from his desk as Clint entered his office.

"Back again?" Burle asked. "The wake over?"

"Hasn't even started yet," Clint said.

"Really?"

"According to Mr. Conlon, the body wasn't ready yesterday," Clint explained.

"Will it be ready today?"

"He says so."

"People must be gettin' impatient."

"If they do, and tempers get short, there could be trouble," Clint said. "Are you ready for that?"

Burle sat back and regarded Clint for a moment.

"Who are you askin' for?" he asked then.

"Just for my own benefit," Clint said.

"Tell me," Burle said, "who else is in town for this wake?"

"You don't know?"

"I know John Wesley Hardin is here. I saw Bat Masterson around town, and Luke Short. Some others. I'm just wonderin' who I missed."

Clint reeled off the names of everybody who had been

in the saloon the night before. "And today, Dutch Craddock rode into town."

"Craddock?" Burle asked. "The bounty hunter?"

"That's right."

"Is he here for the wake?"

"He says no," Clint said, "so that means he's here to collect on somebody."

"If that's the case," Burle said, "he'll be comin' in to see me eventually."

"I suppose so," Clint said. "If that's the way he does business."

"It's the way he's supposed to do business," Burle said.

"Well," Clint said, "with all the short tempers and quick trigger fingers in town, I was just wondering if you were prepared. You know, if you had deputies?"

"Why? Do you want to volunteer?"

"Not at all," Clint said. "Like I said, I was just wondering."

"Well, Mr. Adams," Burle said, "let me assure you that I know how to do my job."

"I hope so," Clint said. "Are you the only law in town? Is there a marshal? A police department?"

"Nope," Burle said. "Just me."

"And . . ."

"If I need deputies," Burle said, "I have them."

"How many?"

"Enough."

"What if I *did* want to volunteer?"

Burle smiled.

"I would say thanks but no thanks, I don't need you," he answered.

"Okay," Clint said, "then I guess you're prepared."

"I am."

"For anything?"

"That's right," Burle said. "For anything."

"If you say so."

Clint started for the door. When he got there, the sheriff said, "Hey."

"Yeah?"

"Thanks for the concern. I appreciate it."

"Sure."

"Now you can tell your friends that you think I know my job."

Clint grinned, opened the door, and said, "I'll tell them."

SEVENTEEN

Clint left the sheriff's office and crossed the street. At that moment he saw Dutch Craddock walk to the door of the sheriff's office and enter. So checking in with the local law was the way he did business.

Clint decided to wait. He found an alley, leaned against the wall, and watched. Ten minutes later Craddock came out. Clint waited until he walked away and was out of sight, then crossed the street and went back in.

"Now what?" the sheriff asked, looking up from his desk.

"I saw Craddock coming in," Clint said. "I waited."

"For what?"

"I'd like to know who he's after."

"Why?" Burle asked. "You want to warn him?"

"Well . . . no, but—" Clint said.

"Okay, look," Burle said, "I'm gonna show this to you, but I don't want to hear it got around town. If it does, I'll know it was you."

"Okay."

"Here." Burle handed Clint a wanted poster.

Clint took it and read it.

"Have you heard of him?"

"Yes."

"Is he here in town?"

Clint handed the poster back.

"There's no way to know for sure."

"Well," Burle said, "if you see him, I'd liked to know about it."

"Of course," Clint said. "If I see him, you'll be the first to know."

Clint turned and headed for the door, but stopped short and turned back.

"Sheriff, that poster. Did you have it among yours, or did Craddock give it to you?"

"He had it on him," Burle said, "and he has many more copies."

"I see," Clint said. "Do you think he'll be showing it around town?"

"I asked him not to," Burle said, "but who knows?"

"Yes," Clint agreed, "who knows?"

Clint decided to stay off the street and get some sleep for a few hours. Once the others—other than he and Bat—were on the streets, anything could happen. And if Burle was sure he had the deputies he needed, there was no need for him to be concerned.

He slept for only two hours, but awoke fairly well refreshed.

And hungry.

He went down to the hotel dining room, and was not surprised to find some of his friends there.

"Gents," he said, "mind if I join you?"

Bat Masterson, Luke Short, and Heck Thomas all welcomed him expansively.

"Get some sleep?" Bat asked as Clint sat.

"Two hours," Clint said, "but it seems to be enough."

The waiter came over and Clint ordered steak and eggs for the second time that day. His companions all seemed to be lunching on beef stew.

"Bat tells us you saw Dutch Craddock ride into town," Heck Thomas said. "Who's he after?"

"I went to the sheriff and found out," Clint said. "Craddock is carrying a sheaf of posters on Tom Horn."

"Horn?" Bat repeated.

"What's Tom done?" Heck asked.

"It has something to do with the Tonto Basin thing in Arizona."

"I thought that was being called the Pleasant Valley War?" Heck said.

"Either way," Luke said, "it had to do with sheep." He made a face.

"Well," Clint said, "somebody's put a price on Tom's head, and Craddock seems to think that Tom is coming here."

"If he does," Heck said, "we can warn him."

"Craddock won't take that well," Clint said. "While we're trying to avoid trouble with the likes of Hardin, Miller, and Allison, we'd be looking for it with Craddock."

"He won't stand against us," Heck said. "Not against all of us."

"Probably not," Clint said. "But Dutch Craddock doesn't want for courage."

"It wouldn't take courage to face us all," Luke Short commented.

"It would be folly," Bat said, "pure folly."

Clint's food came and they all fell to eating in silence for a time.

EIGHTEEN

"Where's Craddock stayin'?" Luke Short asked over coffee.

"Here," Clint said.

"Maybe we should go and talk to him," the gambler said.

"About what?" Clint asked. "You think you're going to talk Craddock out of doing his job?"

"Not a chance," Bat Masterson said.

"Besides," Heck said, "if there's a bounty on Horn, Craddock won't be the only man after it."

"What did it say Horn was wanted for, Clint?" Masterson asked.

"The poster said murder."

"Oh," Masterson said.

"Only I know Horn's not a killer."

"He's not?" Heck Thomas asked.

"Okay," Clint said, "let's put it this way. He's not a murderer."

Nobody offered an argument.

"So what do we do?" Bat asked. "Just let him ride in and face Craddock?"

"Isn't that what Tom Horn would choose to do?" Clint asked.

"It's exactly what he'd do," Heck said.

"He wouldn't appreciate us horning in," Short said. "*No* joke intended."

"In any case," Clint said, "I'll just keep an eye out for his arrival."

"Maybe he won't even come," Bat said.

"With all the gunhands who have already arrived?" Luke Short said. "I would bet that he does come."

"No bet," Bat said.

"Me neither," Clint said.

"Well," Short said, pushing his empty coffee cup away, "I've got to buy a new suit for the wake."

"I'll come with you," Heck said.

"You?" Short asked.

They'd make an odd couple, indeed, since Luke Short was always impeccably dressed in dark three-piece suits, often accompanied by a silk top hat, while Heck Thomas favored more common trail clothes.

"I could use a new hat," Heck said.

"At least," Short said.

"With all the itchy trigger fingers in town," Clint said, "we're probably wise to travel in twos."

"Good point," Short said. "I'll be glad of your company, Heck."

Heck was looking down at his clothes, no doubt wondering what Short meant by his "at least" comment. The two men rose and left the dining room and the hotel.

Clint poured himself another cup of coffee, and Bat nudged his cup over for the rest.

"They left us with the check," he observed.

"What else is new?" Clint asked.

"More coffee, sir?" the waiter asked Clint.

"No," Clint replied, "just the check."

"For the others, too?" the waiter asked.

"Yes," Clint said, "I'll pay for everyone."

"With my thanks," Bat said, toasting Clint with his coffee cup.

Clint ignored the toast and took out his money.

Outside the hotel, Clint and Bat studied the crowded streets. It was now midday, and all of the men who had come to town for the wake were probably up and about.

But where?

As if in answer to the question, shots suddenly rang out. Several of them.

"Where?" Bat asked.

"There!" Clint pointed.

They ran in that direction. After two blocks they saw a crowd, and went to join them. In the center was Jim Miller, standing over two dead men with his gun still in his hand.

Clint stepped into the circle made by the crowd, to join Miller.

"Jim?" he said.

Miller turned his head to look at him.

"What happened?" Clint asked.

"These two were lookin' to make a name for themselves at my expense," Miller said. "It was a bad idea."

"Obviously," Clint said. "I think you can holster your gun now."

Miller gave the suggestion some thought, then holstered his weapon. Suddenly, the sheriff appeared from the crowd.

"What happened here?" he demanded. "Who killed these men?"

"I did," Miller said.

"Why?"

"They asked for it."

"And you are?"

"Jim Miller."

Somebody in the crowd shouted, "Killin' Jim Miller!"

Miller ignored the name.

Sheriff Burle leaned over to inspect the two men, then straightened.

"Both dead, shot once."

"It usually takes only one," Miller offered.

"These were not gunmen," Burle said. "They work around here."

"That one's gun is on the ground next to him," Clint pointed out.

"So it is," Burle said. He looked around. "All right, that's enough. Go back to what you were doing. Not you, Benson. Get a few men and take these bodies over to the undertaker."

"Sure, Sheriff," Benson said.

"Mr. Miller," Burle said, "I'll need you to come to my office." He put his hand out. "And I'll need your gun."

Clint didn't know Miller well enough to predict his reaction. But he'd heard enough about him so he wasn't surprised by it.

"I'll come with you and answer your questions," Miller said, "but you ain't gettin' my gun."

J. Burle stared at Miller, then looked at Clint, but for what?

"It sounds fair to me," Clint said. "If he gives up his gun, he's a target."

"While in my custody?"

"Is he under arrest?"

"Well, no."

"Then he's not in your custody, is he?"

Burle frowned, then looked at Miller.

"All right," he said to the gunfighter. "Let's go to my office."

Miller looked at Clint, then turned and followed the sheriff to his office.

Bat stepped up and stood next to Clint while a group of men lifted the dead bodies and carried them off. Before long, the street was no more crowded than on a regular busy day.

"Looks like it's starting," Bat said.

"Yep."

"Think Miller had call for this?"

"I don't know," Clint said, "but then we don't have to, do we? We're not wearing badges."

"No," Bat said, "we're not."

"Still," Clint said, "let's keep a sharp eye out. This might just be the beginning."

NINETEEN

Rather than go to the Crystal Queen for a drink, Clint took Bat Masterson to the Buckskin, where bartender Kelly O'Day greeted him warmly.

"Hey, I heard the shootin'," he said. "That wasn't you, was it?"

"No, not me or my friend here," Clint said. "Kelly, this is Bat Masterson. How about a beer for each of us?"

"Comin' up," O'Day said. "Pleased to have ya both in my place."

He drew two beers and set them on the bar.

"On the house," he said, leaning his elbows on the bar. "Come on, tell me, who was shootin'?"

Clint looked at Bat, who just shrugged.

"It was Jim Miller," Clint said. "Apparently two locals wanted to try their luck."

"And they didn't fare very well," Bat said.

"Miller?" O'Day said. "Aw, damn!"

"Why?" Clint asked.

"I didn't have him in the pool."

"What pool?" Clint asked.

"The bettin' pool," the bartender said. "I picked you to be the first one to kill somebody."

Clint stared at the man and Bat said, "I think you better walk away, friend."

"Hey, uh, I didn't mean nothin'—"

"Walk away," Bat said again. This time the man obeyed.

Clint sipped his beer, then made a face and slammed it down on the bar so that it spilled.

"Lost my thirst," he said. "For this place anyway."

"Me, too," Bat said. "We might as well go over to the Crystal and see what's goin' on."

Clint nodded and the two men left the saloon.

One of the other men in the saloon walked up to the bar and asked O'Day, "What was that all about?"

"Beats me," O'Day said. "That was Clint Adams and Bat Masterson. All I did was tell 'em about the bettin' pool and they got all upset and left."

"You gonna dump those beers out?" the man asked.

"Yeah, unless you want 'em."

"We'll take 'em," the man said. He grabbed the two beers left by Clint Adams and Bat Masterson and carried them back to his table. He set one down in front of his partner.

"Was that them?" Cleve Johnson asked.

"Yeah," Steve Carter said, "it was them."

"Who's beer do I got?" Johnson asked.

"That one was Masterson's."

"I want the Gunsmith's."

Carter shrugged, switched beers with Johnson. He didn't care. There was more beer in Masterson's mug anyway.

"Whataya think they got all mad about?" Johnson asked.

"Seems like they don't like bein' bet on."

"I ain't too happy with the pool neither," Johnson said. "I had me John Wesley Hardin. Damn Miller."

"I had Clay Allison."

"I wonder who Miller killed."

"What's it matter?" Johnson asked.

"I'm just thinkin' . . ."

"Uh-oh," Johnson said. "That's never a good sign. We always get in trouble when you start thinkin.'" "Naw, naw, just hear me out."

"All right," Johnson said with a deep sigh, "go ahead. After all, you did get me a free beer."

"With all these big reps in town," Carter said, "we got us an opportunity . . ."

TWENTY

Clint and Bat entered the Crystal Queen and weren't surprised to find it as packed as the day before, perhaps even more.

"See anybody?" Clint asked.

"Hardin at the bar," Bat said, "further down Allison."

"I see Baca at a table."

"What about Heck and Luke?"

"Not here," Clint said. "Let's get a drink."

They went up to the bar and elbowed open two places for themselves. This time when they got two beers, they kept quiet and drank them.

And then he walked in.

Craddock.

It was as if everyone in the saloon recognized him, and wondered if they were on his list. Craddock was known as a man who always brought home his prey. If you were on his list, you were as good as dead.

Clint, Bat, and the absent Heck Thomas, Bass Reeves, and Luke Short were the only ones who knew who he was really after.

Clint looked down the bar at John Wesley Hardin and Clay Allison. Both men seemed very calm.

"Must be no paper out on those boys," Clint said. "They know Craddock's not after them."

"Maybe they just know they can take him," Heck suggested.

"Does anybody know that?" Clint asked.

"Well . . . you can take him, can't you?" Bat asked.

"I don't know," Clint said, "and I'm not looking to find out."

"Have you ever seen his move?" Luke Short asked.

"I don't have to," Clint said. "He's a killer, pure and simple. You never want to face a man who kills for a living. And maybe for pleasure."

Craddock examined the room, then moved to the bar. A space cleared for him somewhere between Clint and John Wesley Hardin, with Clay Allison the farthest away from him.

Craddock got a beer placed in front of him, leaned on the bar, and sipped it. Suddenly, from the other end of the bar, Clay Allison pushed away from it and walked down to where Craddock was standing.

"Now," Heck Thomas said, "I wonder what this is about."

Allison had no trouble securing a place next to Craddock because nobody else wanted it.

"Craddock," he said.

"Clay."

"You still owe me a drink."

"Do I?"

"From Waco, remember?"

"Oh yeah," Craddock said, making a face.

"You forgot?"

Craddock looked at Clay Allison.

"Nobody likes to remember having to have his life saved," Craddock said. "What are you drinkin'?"

"A beer."

Dutch Craddock waved to the bartender, who brought a beer over.

"How long have you been here?" Craddock asked.

"Since yesterday," Allison said. "Came for the wake. Is that why you're here?"

"I didn't know anything about a wake until Clint Adams told me."

"When did you see Adams?"

"Just today, when I rode in."

"Was that a happy . . . reunion?"

"No reunion," Craddock said.

"So you're not friends with Adams?"

"No," Craddock said, then looked at Allison and added, "Not friends with you either, as I recall."

"No," Allison said, "that's how I remember it, too."

But he didn't move from his place. As Craddock had bought him the beer, he decided to finish it there, in the man's company.

"So, if you're not here for the wake, you must be huntin' somebody."

"I'm always hunting somebody."

"Who is it this time?" Allison asked. "Anybody in this saloon?"

"Not anyone I saw when I walked in," Craddock said. "Not you, Allison."

"Hardin?"

"I saw him when I walked in," Craddock said. "I have no paper on him."

"Jim Miller, then," Allison said. "He killed two men in the street today."

"Then he's the problem of the local law, not mine," Craddock said.

"So who is it, then?"

"Not your worry," Craddock said.

"Oh, don't worry," Allison said, "I wouldn't warn him."

"This way," Craddock said, "you won't even be tempted."

"Good point."

"Finish your beer and let me be, Allison," Craddock said. "We're even now."

"Well," Allison said, "if one beer is the value you put on your life, then yeah, we're even."

When Craddock didn't reply, Allison shrugged and took his beer back to his place at the bar. Before he got there, though, he was stopped by John Wesley Hardin.

"Get anythin' out of him?"

Allison raised his mug and said, "Just a beer he owed me for savin' his life."

"Is that what his life is worth?"

"I guess so."

"Is he here for the wake?"

"No," Allison said. "I got that much out of him, at least. He didn't know anythin' about the wake until Clint Adams told him."

"Hmmm," Hardin said.

Allison moved on, reclaimed his former place at the bar.

"That didn't look like a happy reunion, did it?" Bat asked.

"Not at all," Clint said, "although it did look like Craddock bought Allison a drink."

"Almost like he owed it to him," Bat said.

"You and I owe each other many drinks," Clint said.

"For saving each other's lives many times over," Bat said. "You think that was it?"

"More than likely," Clint said. "They didn't look like friends."

"Why don't the two of you stop talking so one of you can go into your deep pockets?" Luke Short said, waving his empty mug.

TWENTY-ONE

Killin' Jim Miller walked into the saloon a short time later to a smattering of applause. Clint didn't know if he was being applauded for killing two men, or for not being in jail.

Whatever the case, he found himself a spot at the already crowded bar and ordered a beer.

Right behind him came Sheriff Burle. He stood inside the batwings, observing the room. When he saw Clint, he walked over.

"Have a beer with us?" Clint asked. "We're waiting for the wake to begin."

"Don't mind if I do," Burle said, "if the rest of your friends don't mind."

"Hell," Heck Thomas said, "belly on up to the bar."

Burle moved up, stood between Clint and Bat, and Clint bought him a beer.

"What'd you get out of Miller?" Bat asked.

"The two men decided to try their luck with him, as he said," Burle said. "He had no choice."

"Any witnesses speak up?" Clint asked.

"Nope," Burle said. "I had to depend on the word of the only living witness or participant."

"Jim Miller," Luke Short said.

"Right."

"You call on any of those deputies yet?" Clint asked.

"Well," Burle said, "that's kind of why I'm here to talk to you boys."

"Count me out," Luke Short said. "Last time I wore a badge, I got into a lot of trouble."

"My deputies are young," Burle said, "and inexperienced."

"They've got to learn sometime," Bat said. "I'm out."

Burle looked at Clint and Heck Thomas.

"All I need is one man to wear a badge and work with them," Burle said. "Show 'em the ropes."

"I'm a rancher now," Heck said. "Just here for a wake."

Burle looked at Clint, who was saved when the batwings swung inward and Bass Reeves walked in, his deputy marshal's badge very prominently displayed on his chest.

"Just in time," Clint said as the big black lawman approached them.

"For what?" Reeves asked.

"Well," Clint said, waving the bartender over, "let's start with a beer."

Moments later, Bass Reeves told Sheriff Burle, "Sure, I'll help out. No problem."

"That's great to hear," Burle said.

"On one condition."

"What's that?" Burle said.

Reeves slapped Clint on the back and said, "Clint, here, has to agree also."

"Now wait—" Clint said.

"Sounds fair to me," Heck Thomas said.

"Me, too," Bat said.

"I'll drink to that," Luke said.

Reeves raised his eyebrows at Clint.

"Yeah, okay," Clint said.

"Okay," Burle said. "Come on over to the office. I'll

introduce you to the other deputies, and give you each a local badge."

"We'll wait here," Bat said with a smile, "hold your places."

"Thanks," Clint said.

Reeves slapped Clint on the back again, and they followed Sheriff Burle out the door.

"What's the big idea?" Clint asked Reeves along the way.

"Come on," Reeves said, "we work good together. Besides, you kinda hung me out to dry on this one, didn't ya?"

Clint hesitated, then said "Yes, well, maybe I did."

"There ya go," Reeves said. "Besides, all we gotta do is back the sheriff up in case of trouble."

"Like with Miller today."

"What happened with Miller?"

Clint told Reeves about the encounter Jim Miller had with two locals in the street.

"You think they pushed him, like he said?" the black marshal asked.

"I guess I don't have any reason to doubt him," Clint said. "After all, I caught three locals eyeing Bat Masterson, figuring to try to rob him."

"I guess the temptation to get a reputation is too big for some people to handle."

"As evidenced by their deaths," Clint said.

They reached the sheriff's office and Burle stopped at the door.

"As I said, my deputies are young," he said to them. "And inexperienced."

"Why not hire more experienced men?" Reeves asked.

"I had two experienced deputies," Burle said, "but they were both killed earlier this year. I have two . . . boys waiting inside."

"Well," Reeves said, "let's have at them, then."

TWENTY-TWO

The two young deputies were impressed to meet not only Bass Reeves, well known as a deputy marshal in the court of the Hanging Judge, but the Gunsmith, as well.

"That's Thad," Burle said, "Thad Burnett, and Billy Cunningham."

Both deputies nodded.

"Boys, Marshal Reeves and Mr. Adams have agreed to help us keep the peace, as long as we have so many visitors in town for the wake."

"That's great," Deputy Cunningham said.

Burle went to his desk, opened a drawer, and took out two badges. He handed one each to Clint and Reeves.

"I propose you each work in tandem with my deputies," he said. "They can learn a lot from each of you. Just making rounds together."

"Sounds good," Clint said.

"I'll put this in my pocket," Reeves said. "No point in wearing two badges."

Clint hesitated, then pinned the badge on.

"Clint, you can team with Thad," Burle said. "He'll show you his rounds."

"Fine."

"Deputy Reeves?"

"Me and Billy, right?" Reeves slapped Billy on the back. Clint knew how hard that big hand could hit, even in camaraderie.

The four deputies left the sheriff's office.

"I'll see you at the Crystal later," Clint said to Reeves, who nodded and followed his young deputy on his rounds.

"Well, Thad," Clint said. "Lead the way."

"Yes, sir."

As they walked, Thad asked, "Is there likely to be a lot of trouble, Mr. Adams?"

"Call me Clint," Clint said, "and with the personalities we have in town, and the lack of judgment your locals have already shown, I'm sure of it."

"We've heard that John Wesley Hardin and Clay Alison are in town, as well as Killin' Jim Miller," Thad said. "Are they likely to start killin'?"

"Not for no reason," Clint said. "But it's likely that someone will try to push them. And that could even happen with men like Bat Masterson and Heck Thomas."

"But they've been lawmen themselves," Thad said.

"That doesn't mean they can't be pushed," Clint said. "And when it comes to getting shot, nobody just stands by and lets it happen."

"Not even you?"

"Especially not me."

Craddock picked out a likely-looking saloon girl and accompanied her up to her room.

Bat Masterson, Luke Short, and Heck Thomas watched him go up.

"I guess he really isn't interested in the wake," Heck said.

"He's probably been on the trail for a long time," Bat said. "We all know what that's like."

"Yeah," Heck said, "a beer, a poke, and then a steak."

"Not necessarily in that order," Luke said, and they laughed.

The three friends turned and faced the bar.

"What do you think?" Bat asked.

"About what?" Heck asked.

"Horn."

"Is he a killer?" Luke asked.

"Tom will kill if he feels it's necessary," Heck said. "How is that any different from the rest of us?"

Craddock followed the girl into her room.

"What's your pleasure, cowboy?" she asked. She turned to face him with her hands on her hips. She was medium height, slender, but with large breasts, which Craddock liked. She looked to be about twenty-five.

"I'm not a cowboy," he said. "Take off your dress."

"No, you ain't," she said. "I heard some talk about you downstairs." She reached behind her to undo her dress.

"Did you?" he said. "What did they say?"

"That you hunt men," she said, letting her dress drop to the floor with a whisper of the fabric on her skin. "That you kill them." She stepped out of the dress and kicked it away. She was naked, her dark brown nipples already puckering.

He knew the talk of killing was getting her excited. He walked past her, took off his gun belt, and hung it on the bedpost, then undid his belt and the buttons of his trousers.

"I kill them when they make me," he said. "When they leave me no choice. Now come over here."

She walked over to him. He could smell her skin, and the wetness between her legs. His own excitement was building.

"Take them down," he said.

She got down on her knees, tugged on his trousers until they and his underwear were around his ankles. His hardening cock sprang out at her, almost hitting her in the nose.

"Suck it," he said.

She smiled at him, wrapped one hand around his cock, and said, "You don't leave me much choice, do you?"

"No," he said, "I don't."

TWENTY-THREE

"So the Crystal Queen is part of your rounds?" Clint asked
Thad.

"Yessir."

"How come I haven't seen you in there today, or yesterday?" Clint asked.

"Um . . ." "Did the sheriff tell you not to go in?"

"No, sir."

"Then what? Were you nervous about going in?"

"Yessir."

"All right, then," Clint said. "Why don't we go inside
together?"

"You and me?"

"That's right."

"Well . . . yessir."

"Good man," Clint said, slapping the young deputy on
the back.

They went through the batwing doors, into the Crystal
Queen.

Bat saw Clint in the mirror, then turned and shielded his
eyes.

"The badge, the badge," he said. "It's too bright."

In point of fact, the badge was sort of tarnished.

"Very funny," Clint said. "This is Deputy Burnett. Thad, this is Luke Short, that's Heck Thomas, and the funny man is Bat Masterson."

"Wow," Thad said. "It's an honor to meet you all." But at the time his eyes were searching the crowd.

"Lookin' for the bad men?" Bat asked.

Thad blushed, looked down, and said, "Well . . ."

"Hardin is halfway down the bar, Clay Allison is all the way at the end," Luke said.

"Where's Craddock?' Clint asked.

"Went upstairs with a girl," Heck said.

"Has Conlon been out?"

"Haven't seen him," Bat said.

"We're getting on toward dusk," Clint said. "He better get this thing started soon or he's going to have a revolt on his hands."

"He's sellin' a lot of whiskey," Heck said.

"Which could be good," Bat said, "or bad."

"For her," Luke said.

Upstairs, the girl, whose name was Delilah, was avidly sucking on what she was thinking of as a killer's cock.

Craddock growled as she gobbled his cock, which, despite its size, she was able to take all the way in. She wet it thoroughly, let it pop from her mouth, then took it in again. Then Craddock got into it, moving his hips, and she simply kept her mouth open and let him fuck it, in and out, in and out . . .

Finally, she cradled his balls in her hand, at the same time teasing his anus with one finger. He reached down and pushed her away.

"None of that!" he said. "Don't touch my asshole!"

"Hey," she said, "whatever you want, sweetie. And you just tell me what you don't want."

"I don't want anybody touchin' my bumhole. Got it?"

"I got it," she said, getting to her feet warily. "Come on, get on the bed, honey. I'll make you feel real good."

She reached down, helped him step out of his pants. She sat him on the bed and took off his boots and socks. When he was completely naked, she got him onto his back. His cock stuck straight up impressively.

"Oh yes," she said, straddling him . . .

"Maybe you should go up and talk to Conlon again," Bat said to Clint.

"Or the woman," Luke said.

"Her name's Alicia," Clint said.

"Oh," Luke said, "excuse me."

"Bat, I think you should go up," Clint said. "I have to finish my rounds with young Thad here."

"Huh?" Thad said. "Oh, uh, yeah, we do."

"See?" Clint said.

"If I go up there," Bat said, "I'll end up killin' the sono-fabitch." He looked at Luke Short.

"Don't look at me," Short said, shaking his head. "I'm very happy to stand here and drink with my friends. Or find a poker game."

Heck silently observed the conversation, keeping out of it while working on his beer. Like Luke Short, he was not becoming impatient with the situation.

"Come on, Thad," Clint said. "We've got work to do."

Clint left his friends to discuss the matter further, went out the batwing doors, pushing the young deputy ahead of him.

TWENTY-FOUR

Craddock pinned the girl to the bed with his hands on her wrists, and his body on hers. She struggled, but only because she thought he wanted her to. She was still excited by being with a man who was known as a killer.

When his penis entered her vagina forcefully, her eyes went wide and she gasped. After that, he began to pound away at her, harder and harder. She knew she was going to be sore, was going to come away from this with bruises and welts, but she didn't care.

Craddock the killer had chosen her!

"Maybe," Bat said to Luke Short and Heck Thomas, "we can sneak back there and get a look at the body."

"To what end?" Luke asked.

"Well, once we're sure he's dead," Bat said, "we can leave."

"Without payin' our respects?" Heck asked.

"Come on," Bat said, "when you think about it, how many of us do you think are actually here to do that? And what does it matter if we see him on our own, or with everyone else when the wake begins?"

"If it begins," Luke said.

"What are you sayin'?" Heck asked.

"What if there's no body?" Luke asked.

"You mean he's not dead?" Heck asked.

"And never was," Bat said. "You know, that's something Conlon would dream up to get himself some business."

"Yeah, but then how does he explain it?" Heck asked.

"He just says he made a mistake," Bat said.

"So you're sayin'," Heck went on, "that there is a body back there, but it's not—"

"Exactly," Luke Short.

"Then he could just as well have said that Clint Adams, the Gunsmith, was dead, and everybody should come to his wake."

"Except that when Clint heard that, he'd come, too," Bat said.

"So you're sayin'—" Heck said.

"Yup," Luke said.

"He could be in here right now," Bat said.

They all turned to face the saloon and scan the crowd with their eyes.

"Well," Bat said, "I guess we're gonna have to get a look at that body."

He turned and waved the bartender over.

"'Nother one?" the man asked.

"Where's the body?"

"Huh?"

"The body for the wake," Bat said. "Where's it bein' kept?"

"Um, well, the back room."

"Is that the room where they're gonna show it?" Luke Short asked.

"No," the bartender said. "They'll bring it from the store-room in the back and put it back there in a room we use for private games."

"Locks on the doors?" Heck asked.

"Yessir."

"Both rooms?" Bat asked.

"Yessir."

"Who's got the keys?"

"Just Mr. Conlon."

"Nobody else?"

"No sir."

"All right," Bat said. "Bring three more beers."

"Yessir."

"So what do you wanna do?" Heck asked. "Break into the back room?"

"That's what I was thinkin'," Bat said. "What about you, Luke?"

"It's against the law," Luke said.

"So?" Bat asked.

"We've got to remember who's wearin' a badge in this town now."

"Right," Bat said, "Clint and Reeves."

"We'd have to figure out a way to handle that," Luke said.

"We could let them in on our plan," Bat said.

"Maybe," Heck suggested, "before we do that, we should actually have a plan."

"Good point," Bat said. "Let's come up with one."

"But what if Conlon is close to opening up the room for the wake?" Heck asked. "Maybe we should find out before we make a move."

"And that would mean Bat going up to talk to him again," Luke said.

"And that means one of you will have to come with me to keep me from killing him."

"I guess that would be me," Heck said.

"Be my guest," Luke said. "I'll take a turn around the saloon, take a look at that back room. Maybe I can see a way to get in."

"All right," Bat said. "We'll meet you back here in twenty minutes."

"Unless you kill Conlon," Luke Short said. "In that case, I'll see you in jail."

TWENTY-FIVE

Clint and Thad finished their rounds without much incident. They had to break up a fight in a small saloon, and settle an argument over a bottle of whiskey in another, but that was all.

"This is the only kind of action I ever see," Thad said as they left the second saloon and started back to the sheriff's office.

"And you want to see another kind?"

"Yes."

"If that was true," Clint said, "then you would have gone into the Crystal Queen before now."

Thad looked down.

"I wanted to, but I was too . . ."

"Frightened?"

"N-No," Thad said. "N-Nervous."

There was only a slight difference, but Clint let the matter drop.

As they entered the sheriff's office, Clint could smell fresh coffee.

"Finished?" Sheriff Burle asked.

"For now," Clint said. "Is that fresh?"

Burle gestured with his white mug and said, "Help yourself."

"Reeves and Billy aren't back yet?" Clint asked, pouring himself a cup. He offered a cup to Thad, who turned it down.

"What do you think of our fair town?" Burle asked.

"It's prospering," Clint said.

"Yes, it is."

"Looks like new buildings are going up all the time."

"They are."

"I would think the town council would allow you some more deputies to police it."

"I've asked," Burle said. "Thad and Billy work for very little. You and Reeves are volunteers."

"More like draftees," Clint said, "but I get your point. But surely, with all the extra guns in town, they would come up with some extra money."

"Well," Burle said, "I've assured them I can handle things."

"And can you?"

"With your help," Burle said, "and the help of Bass Reeves, yes."

"But what if we decided to leave town?" Clint asked. "And take our friends with us?"

"Then that would reduce the number of guns in town, wouldn't it?" Burle asked.

"You have a point," Clint said. "If we all left town, things would be less tense."

"But John Wesley Hardin, Jim Miller, and Clay Allison would still be here," Thad pointed out. "And many of the others."

"Like Craddock," Clint said.

Burle sat back in his chair.

"I expect most of the trouble to come from him," the lawman said.

"If Tom Horn arrives in town," Clint said.

"And who knows who else will arrive?" Thad asked.

"It's dark," Burle said. "When Reeves and Billy come back, three of you should go and get some supper. Thad, you and Billy decide who will stay here at the office."

"Yessir."

"Tell me something, Sheriff," Clint said.

"What's that?"

"Conlon," Clint said. "Who works for him?"

"He's got lots of employees."

"Yes, but any guns?"

"Plenty," Sheriff Burle said. "He calls them his security force."

"I haven't seen any of them."

"That's because he's got them guarding the body," Burle said, "until it's time for the wake."

"Whenever that will be," Clint said.

"Well, whenever it is," Burle said, "whenever he puts the body on display, his men will be guarding it."

"But they're guarding it now, right?"

"Yes."

"So if someone got impatient, and tried to see the body ahead of time, they'd stop them, right?"

"And if I know those men—and I do—they wouldn't just stop them. They're led by a man named Trench."

"Trench?" Clint said. "That name sounds familiar. Trench . . ."

"He had a reputation," Burle said. "Before he came here months ago . . ."

"Yes," Clint said "A rep with his gun."

"Fast and deadly," Burle said. "That's what they say about him."

"And about a lot of the men who are here in town," Clint said. "With Trench guarding the body, there's bound to be trouble."

"I think so."

Clint put his cup down on the desk and stood up.

"When Bass comes back, tell him I've gone to the Crystal Queen."

"To do what?" Burle asked.

"To make sure that nobody gets impatient," Clint said.

TWENTY-SIX

Bat Masterson and Heck Thomas went up the stairs to Ben Conlon's office. Heck knocked, and they waited. The door was opened by Conlon himself.

"Masterson," Conlon said, then looked at Heck. "What happened to Adams?"

"He's busy. Can we come in?"

"Sure," Conlon said. He backed away and allowed them to enter. "Close the door, please."

Bat closed it.

"Who's your friend?"

"Heck Thomas," Heck said, introducing himself.

"Ah, the famous detective. And what are you detecting today?"

"I'm tryin' to find out when the wake is gonna start," Heck said.

"Me, too," Conlon said.

"What's that mean?" Bat asked.

"I'm looking for my undertaker," Conlon said. He shrugged. "Can't find him."

"Why don't you just wheel the body out, then?" Bat asked. "Let everybody have a look?"

"I can't," Conlon said. "I'm no expert. I don't know if the body is ready to be viewed."

"All right, then," Bat said, "just let us have a look. Then we can be on our way."

"Oh, I can't do that, Bat," Conlon said.

"Why not?"

"If I do it for you, I'll have to do it for everyone downstairs."

"We won't tell them," Heck said.

"You'll tell your friends," Conlon said, "and they'll tell someone. It would get out. And then I'd be in a lot of trouble." Conlon sat down behind his desk. "I just can't do it, Bat. Sorry."

"That's okay," Bat said. "I figured you'd say that. We'll get out of your way."

Bat and Heck headed for the door.

"So what are you gonna do?" Conlon asked.

Bat opened the door, turned, and looked at the saloon owner.

"I can't tell you, Conlon," he said. "If I do, I'd have to tell everybody downstairs . . . wouldn't I?"

TWENTY-SEVEN

Clint entered the saloon, looked around, spotted Luke Short at the bar.

"Where are Bat and Heck?"

"They went up to see Conlon," Luke said. "They're gonna try to find out when the wake will start."

"And what are they planning if Conlon says it's not going to start soon?"

"We're comin' up with a plan to get a look at the body," Luke said. "I checked the back room, it looks easy enough to get into."

"Yeah, but maybe not so easy to get out—alive."

"Whataya mean?"

"The sheriff told me that Conlon has a security force," Clint said. "Headed up by a man named Trench."

"Trench. I know that name. This is not good."

"We've got to keep Bat and Heck from doing something stupid."

"Don't worry."

"What do you mean?"

"They wouldn't dare do somethin' stupid without me."

Bat and Heck Thomas did not go back to the bar. Instead, they looked for a way to get to the rear of the building. Heck found a door that was locked, decided to see if there was any entry from outside.

In the alley behind the saloon they found another door, also locked. It was pitch black and Heck produced a lucifer and scratched it to life.

"Can you get this open?" Bat asked.

"Do I look like a burglar?" Heck asked.

"You look like a guy with a big, burly shoulder."

Heck put that shoulder to the door and tested it.

"This is a solid door," he said, "much more than most back doors."

"There must be somethin' inside they don't want anybody to see," Bat reasoned.

"I'd say," Heck agreed.

"Okay," Bat said, looking the building over, squinting at the windows, which were blocked from inside. "We can find a way in. We can figure this out."

"Break a window?"

"I'd like to get in without anyone hearin' us," Bat said. "Or even knowing that we'd been in there."

"Now you tell me," Heck said, striking another match.

Clint and Luke made their way through the crowded saloon to the back, looking for a way to get to the storeroom where the body was being held.

"This is locked," Luke said.

"And unguarded."

"So there's either nothing inside," Luke said, "or the guards are inside."

"I vote nothing," Clint said. "Come on, let's find the storeroom."

They found a hallway that led to another door—also locked.

"Outside," Clint said, pointing farther down the hall.

They went to the end of the hall, found another door which led to the alley in the back. There they found Bat Masterson and Heck Thomas about to force a locked door open. Heck was holding a match to try to illuminate the scene.

"Wait!" Clint hissed.

The two men stopped short and looked at him.

"What's wrong?" Bat asked. "You gonna arrest us? We think the body is in here."

"Yeah," Clint said, "and so are a bunch of guards."

"What?" Heck asked.

"Come back inside with us and we'll tell you what," Clint said.

"But—" Bat said.

"Trust us," Luke said. "We're keepin' you from makin' a big mistake."

As Clint and Luke brought Bat Masterson and Heck Thomas back into the saloon, a table in the back suddenly opened up.

"Grab that!" Clint barked. "I'll get some beers."

He went to the bar, got four mugs of beer, and managed to wrangle them back to the table his friends had claimed. He set the beers down in the center of the table, and sat. They all grabbed one.

"Now what's goin' on?" Bat asked after a healthy drink.

"You know a man named Trench?" Clint asked.

"I know of him," Bat said.

"Well, he's working for Conlon," Clint said.

"As what?"

"Security chief," Clint said. "Apparently, he's got some guards on the body."

"Not outside the room," Heck said, "so they must be . . . inside."

"Right."

"That would not have been fun," Bat Masterson said, "breaking into a room full of guards."

"Did you talk to Conlon?" Clint asked.

"Yes," Bat said. "He's still putting the wake off, blaming the undertaker."

"He says he can't find him," Heck added.

"Maybe," Clint suggested, *"we* should try to find him."

"Tonight?" Luke asked.

"I don't think anything's going to happen tonight," Clint said, "but early tomorrow morning for sure. Let's find out what he has to say about things."

"Anybody know his name?" Luke asked.

"No," Clint said, "but we'll find out tomorrow."

"You got more rounds to do tonight?" Bat asked.

"No," Clint said, "I get to eat and go back to work in the morning."

"I guess we're done here for the day, then," Bat said. "I'm going back to my hotel room."

"No poker?" Heck asked.

"Not tonight."

"You, Luke?" Heck asked.

"Yeah, I got a game," Luke said, frowning, "if I can just remember where."

TWENTY-EIGHT

They left their table and began to go their own ways when Bass Reeves walked in.

"Hey, hey," he said, "the party's over?"

"I'm turning in," Bat said.

"I've got a poker game," Luke said.

"I've got nothin' to do," Heck said.

"I can stay for a beer and fill you in," Clint said. "Where's your deputy?"

"Billy is getting somethin' to eat," Reeves said. "Then he's gonna go back and relieve Thad."

"So you're done for the night?" Clint asked.

Reeves nodded and said, "Same as you."

The three friends walked over to the bar as Bat and Luke went out the batwings.

When they all had beers, they turned to lean against the bar with their elbows, facing the room. They saw Elfego Baca walking up to them.

"I see something new has occurred," he said happily.

"We're just tryin' to help out," Reeves said.

"Bass made me do it," Clint said.

Baca looked at Heck Thomas, who shrugged and said, "Nobody made me do it."

Baca waved to the bartender for a beer.

"I am assuming you gentlemen know when this wake is going to take place," the young Mexican lawman said.

"We know when it's not taking place," Clint said.

"Anytime soon," Reeves said.

"Is that a fact?" Baca asked, accepting his beer from the barman. "I am afraid I cannot stay much longer."

"As a matter of fact," Reeves said, "neither can I."

"Well," Clint said, "we're going to get to the bottom of it tomorrow."

"Very well," Baca said, "one more day." He started to walk back to his table, then turned around again. "If you need any help, let me know."

"We'll keep that in mind," Clint said. *"Gracias."*

Elfego Baca returned to his table.

"Think the others will be as patient as he's being?" Reeves asked.

"Maybe not," Clint said. "John Wesley Hardin is not known for his patience."

"Neither are Jim Miller or Clay Allison," Heck Thomas said.

"They'll have to be," Clint said, "at least for tonight. Tomorrow we'll get some answers."

They clinked their glasses and drank.

Jim Miller saw the badges Clint Adams and Bass Reeves were wearing. He waited until they finished their beers with Heck Thomas and all three left the room, then he walked down to where John Wesley Hardin was standing.

"You see the badges?"

Hardin turned and looked at him. "On Adams and Reeves? Yeah."

"What do you suppose that's about?"

"Who knows?" Hardin asked. "Maybe they miss wearin' tin."

"I don't like it."

"You got any paper out on you now?"

"No."

"Then what are you worried about?"

"I'm always worried," Miller said. "I thought you and me were the same way."

"You and me," John Wesley Hardin said, "isn't alike, at all. Go talk to Allison."

"Clay Allison's crazy."

"Funny," Hardin said, "that's what I always heard about you."

Miller stared at him with dead eyes, then turned and walked away. As far as Hardin was concerned, Miller and Allison were alike, and he was like neither of them. Let them worry together.

He went back to his beer.

"Don't you ever get tired?" the girl asked Craddock.

"No," he said. He was lying on his back on the bed with his hands behind his head, still naked. She was lying next to him, trying to catch her breath. His beautiful penis was still half hard, even after he'd used it on her half a dozen times. It was beautiful, but at the moment she saw it as another weapon of his, and she didn't want him using it on her again anytime soon.

She needed some rest.

"Tell me about the wake," he said.

Oh good, she thought. He finally wants to talk.

"What about it?"

"When's it supposed to start?"

"Yesterday."

"What's the holdup?"

"I don't know," she said.

He reached out, slid his hand down her belly until he could tangle his hand in her bush. Then he pulled.

"Ow! What the—"

"When is the wake?"

"It was supposed to start yesterday," she said. "That's all I know."

"Who's in charge?"

"Conlon, Ben Conlon."

"Who is he?"

"My boss. He owns this place."

"What's his agenda?"

"Agenda?"

"What's he after?"

"What else?" she asked. "Money."

"So he's figured out a way for this wake to make him money?"

"I'll bet."

"He's your direct boss?"

"No, that's Alicia," Delilah said. "Alicia Simmons. She runs the girls."

"She belong to Conlon?"

"Maybe he thinks so, but no."

He released the hold he had on her pubic hair, but left his hand there. In minutes he was asleep.

TWENTY-NINE

Miller moved up next to Allison. Two men moved away to give him room.

"Did you see Clint Adams and Bass Reeves?" he asked Allison.

"What about them?"

"They're wearin' badges."

"That's not news," Allison said. "Reeves is a deputy marshal."

"They're wearin' local badges."

Allison finally looked at Miller.

"What's that about?"

"That's what I'm wonderin'."

Allison looked around.

"Are they still here?"

"No, they left."

"Any lawmen in the place?"

"No locals," Miller said. "Baca is still here."

"Is he wearin' a badge?"

"Yeah, from somewhere in New Mexico."

Allison turned his attention back to his drink.

"Have a beer," he said. "Nothin's gonna happen until tomorrow."

"I don't like this," Miller said. "The wake was supposed to be today."

"If you're impatient, leave," Allison said.

"Not a chance," Miller said. "I wanna make sure the bastard is really dead."

"Then we have to wait it out," Allison said.

Delilah rolled over to get off the bed. As she did, Craddock grabbed her wrist.

"Where are you goin'?" he asked.

"I have to go back to work."

"No," Craddock said.

"Look, love," she said, "if I don't work, I don't get paid."

"I'll pay you for the night."

"The whole night?"

"Yeah."

"You mean you want to—"

"I want to sleep," he said. "You want to sleep?"

"I'd love to sleep," she said. "I don't hardly ever get a good night's sleep."

"Okay then," she said, sliding back onto the bed next to him. She rolled over, facing away from him. "Good night."

But he was already asleep again.

Clint and Bat got back to their hotel and split up in the lobby. Their rooms were on different floors.

"Craddock is stayin' here, right?" Bat asked.

"That's right."

"Did you see him leave the saloon?"

"No," Clint said, "I didn't."

"I hope nothin' happens tonight," Bat said. "I'm tired."

Clint was tired, too. He hadn't slept all that much the day before.

"I'll meet you down here for breakfast," he told Bat.

"Okay," Bat said, "but not too early, okay?"

They settled on a time and went to their rooms.

* * *

Conlon walked down to Alicia's room and knocked. When she answered, he tried to look past her into her room.

"Are you alone?"

"Why wouldn't I be?" she asked.

"I was just wondering," he said. "Can I come in?"

"I'm really tired, Ben."

"Is that your way of telling me there really is someone in there with you?"

"No," she said, "it's my way of tellin' you that I'm tired."

"Is it Adams?" he demanded. "Is he in there with you? Is that why you won't let me in?"

"Why would you think that?"

"Because I know you had him in there once before," he told her.

"Well, he's not in here tonight. Good night, Ben."

She closed the door in his face. He owned the saloon, he owned the buildings, and he owned her. What he should have done was kick the door in and take her.

What he did was turn and walk back down the hall to his office.

Alicia waited until she felt sure that Conlon was in his office, then picked up her wrap and walked to the door. Clint Adams may not have been in her room, but Conlon demanding to know if he was gave her an idea.

She cracked the door and peered out. When she didn't see Conlon lurking about, she stepped out and closed her door gently behind her. She went to the stairs, walked down, and slipped out the back door.

THIRTY

Clint was trying to decide whether to reread a Twain or a Poe when there was a knock on his door. His holster was hanging on the bedpost. He grabbed the gun and carried it to the door with him.

"Who is it?" he asked.

"Alicia."

He opened the door, holding the gun behind his back with his left. She was standing in the hall, alone.

"It's just me," she said, putting her hands up. "I didn't bring any gunmen."

He opened the door all the way and said, "Come in."

She stepped past him. As she did, he stuck his head out and looked both ways.

"Worried about my reputation?" she asked him as he closed the door.

"Are you?"

"No."

"Then I'm not either," he said.

He walked to the bedpost and holstered the gun, then turned to face her. He was bare-chested and barefooted, wearing only his trousers.

"What brings you here, Alicia?"

"What do you think?"

She tossed her wrap away, reached behind her to undo her dress, and let it drop to the floor. It was a practiced move Clint had seen many women do before—saloon girls, whores, and women who simply wanted to impress.

He was impressed.

Three men sitting in the saloon were having a similar conversation to what Bat Masterson and Heck Thomas had been talking about.

"I'm getting tired of waitin' for this wake," Teddy McCain said. "How about you guys?"

"Yeah," Dick Dutrow said. "We seen enough famous guns walkin' around here in the past two days."

"So whatta we do?" Andy Thomas asked.

McCain looked around. "Looks like most of the lawmen quit for the night."

"Yeah, but the others are still here," Dutrow said. "Allison, Hardin, and Jim Miller."

"They won't get in our way," McCain said.

"Way of what?" Thomas asked. "Whatta we gonna do?"

"We," McCain said, "are gonna get a look at the body."

"How do we do that?" Dutrow asked.

"I heard some talk that the body is locked in a storeroom in the back," McCain said. "They're waitin' for word from the undertaker before they bring it out."

"So?"

"So we're gonna go in and take a look."

"How?" Dutrow asked.

McCain looked at his two partners and said, "Come on, boys. It's only a lock."

Clint approached Alicia and cradled her two perfect handfuls of breasts in his palms. He squeezed them, popped the nipples with his thumbs while she sighed and dropped her head back. He leaned over to touch each nipple with the tip of his tongue. He licked them until they were distended, then took them and worried them between his teeth. She moaned and put her hands behind his head to hold him there—and then they heard the barrage of shots.

He jerked his head up and looked at her.

"Forget it," she said. "Probably some drunk cowboys. Let the law handle it."

"The problem is," he said, grabbing his shirt, "for the time being, I am the law."

As he put his shirt on, she saw the light glint off the badge pinned to it.

"Oh," she said.

He pulled on his boots, grabbed his gun belt, and said, "If you're here when I get back, we can continue."

"Well, okay—"

But Clint was out the door.

When Clint hit the street, he saw people running toward the Crystal. It didn't surprise him that the large saloon was the source of the shooting. He only hoped Alicia was right, and it was just drunk cowboys.

When he got to the saloon, he had his gun belt strapped on, and his shirt buttoned. He entered through the batwing doors and the occupants of the saloon turned to look at him.

"In the back," somebody said, and a few men pointed the way.

"It's the storeroom," a saloon girl said.

Of course it is, Clint thought.

THIRTY-ONE

Clint reached the inner door to the storeroom, which was wide open. Inside was a coffin, with the lid on it, and four men wearing some sort of uniform. On the floor were three other men, bleeding profusely, and dead.

"Hold it!" a man said to him.

Clint turned to the man. He was in his forties, broad shoulders, dressed in the same dark clothes as the other guards, but while they wore silver badges, he wore a gold one.

"Who are you?" he asked.

"Trench," the man said. "Head of security. These are my men."

"Did you shoot these men?" Clint asked.

"We did."

"Why?"

"They forced the door and attempted to enter," Trench said. "We have orders to keep anyone from coming inside."

"By killing them?"

"By any means necessary."

Clint heard someone behind him, turned, and saw Bass Reeves coming toward him, followed by Deputy Billy, and finally, Sheriff Burle himself.

"What's goin' on?" Burle demanded.

"Your security men killed these three men," Clint said, pointing, "because they tried to enter this room."

"Which was locked and off-limits to customers," Trench added.

"Any witnesses?" Burle asked.

"Just me and my men," Trench said.

"Well," Burle said, "I'm going to need you and your men to hand over your guns and come to my office with me and my deputies."

"That's not a problem—" Trench started.

"Good. Let's—"

"As long as we wait until I can get some more of my men down here to guard this room."

"You have more men?" Burle asked.

"I do."

Burle looked at Clint, then at Reeves, who shrugged.

"I say no," Clint said. "Let's take them in now."

"I can't allow that," Trench said.

"You'd resist?" Burle asked.

"Forcefully," Trench assured him.

Burle looked at Clint.

"We don't need another shooting in this hallway," he said. "We'll wait for him to get some more men down here."

"Fine," Clint said.

"Meanwhile," Burle said, "Billy? Go out into the saloon and get some men to carry these men over to the undertaker's."

"I'd like to come along," Clint said.

Burle looked at him.

"To the undertaker's," Clint added.

"Why?"

"I have some questions for the undertaker," Clint said, "who seems to be missing."

"Missing?" Burle asked. "I don't know anything about that."

"Well," Clint said, "I'll find out. What's the undertaker's name?"

"Driscoll," Burle said. "Henry Driscoll."

"Billy," Clint said, "let's get those men to carry these bodies."

"Yessir."

"I'll stay here with the sheriff," Reeves said.

Clint nodded. As he and Billy walked away, he heard Burle say, "All right, Mr. Trench—"

"Captain Trench."

"Let's have those weapons and then you can fetch your other men."

THIRTY-TWO

Clint followed the townsmen who were carrying the three dead bodies to the undertaker's office. When they got there, the men looked at him and he stepped forward to pound on the man's locked door. He had to knock again before a light appeared inside.

"I'm comin', I'm comin'!" a man shouted.

The door opened and a man appeared.

"Are you the undertaker?" Clint asked.

"Yeah, that's him!" one of the townsmen said. "The sheriff tol' us to bring these bodies here."

"Okay, okay," the man said. "Bring 'em in."

He stepped aside and the men carried the bodies inside. The undertaker was in his sixties, tall with snow white air. His eyes were watery, probably because they had jarred him from a deep sleep.

"Take 'em in the back."

The man turned and looked at Clint.

"New deputy?" he asked.

"Temporary," Clint said. "Are you Henry Driscoll?"

"That's me," the undertaker said. "And you?"

"Clint Adams."

"The Gunsmith? That Clint Adams?"

"That's right. Listen, there are a lot of people waiting for the wake to take place."

"The wake?"

"At the Crystal Queen."

"Why tell me?"

"Well, Mr. Conlon told me the wake was being held up by you," Clint said. "That he can't put the body on display until you clear it."

"I've got nothin' to do with Mr. Conlon's business," Driscoll said. "If he told you that, he's lyin' to you."

"Why doesn't that surprise me?" Clint said. "Okay, Mr. Driscoll, thanks."

"Hey," Driscoll said, "where were these men killed?"

"At the Crystal."

"Why doesn't that surprise me?"

Now convinced that there was no good reason for the holdup of the wake, Clint headed back to the Crystal. But when he arrived there, he found the place locked up tight. He wondered how they'd managed to get everyone out so quickly.

He changed direction and walked to the sheriff's office.

When he entered the office, he found Sheriff Burle behind his desk, with Billy on one side and Bass Reeves on the other. The other deputy, Thad, was nowhere to be seen.

Sitting in front of the desk were Trench and one of his men. The other two men were standing behind them.

"You get the bodies taken care of?" Burle asked Clint.

"Yeah, we got them stowed away for the night."

"And the undertaker? Driscoll?" Burle asked. "Is he missing?"

"Nope," Clint said, "he was there—and he doesn't know anything about the wake or why it hasn't started."

"Then Conlon's been lyin' to us," Reeves said.

"Oh, yeah," Clint said. "And I'm going to ask him about it tomorrow."

"Well, before we get to that," Burle said, "let's finish up with tonight."

"Fine," Clint said. "I was surprised to find the Crystal closed when I got back."

"I didn't want anybody else gettin' shot tonight," Burle said. He looked at Trench. "I want to know what exactly your job is, Trench."

"Security," Trench said.

"Can you be a little more specific?"

"You'd have to ask Mr. Conlon about that," Trench said. "He told me I'm in charge of security."

"And what does that mean to you?"

"That I can do whatever I want to keep Mr. Conlon, his employees, and his saloon safe and secure."

"And is that what you feel you did tonight?" Burle asked him.

"Definitely," Trench said. "Mr. Conlon especially wants that room to stay secure until the wake starts."

"And when will that be?" Burle asked.

"I don't know anything about that," Trench said.

"Well, why haven't I seen you in town before?" Burle asked. "Or know about your job at the Crystal?"

"Again," Trench said, "you'd have to ask Mr. Conlon about that."

"Don't worry," Burle said, "I intend to."

"Can me and my men go?" Trench asked.

"You can leave this office," Burle said, "but don't leave town."

"Why would we do that?" Trench asked, standing up. "We've got a job to do."

Trench stood up and turned, found himself face-to-face with Clint, who didn't move. The tension was thick as all the other men in the room watched them. They stood that way for a few seconds, and then Trench stepped around him.

Trench's men followed him out the door.

"Wasn't there any way you could hold them responsible for what they did?"

"Marshal?" Burle said to Bass Reeves. "You want to explain it?"

"They tried to enter a section of the saloon that was off-limits to customers," Reeves said. "And they forced a locked door."

"But they had the right to kill them?" Clint asked.

"They were armed," Reeves said, "and according to Trench, they drew their guns."

"You have to take his word for it?"

"His men backed his story," Burle said, "and there were no other witnesses. But don't worry. I'm gonna have a talk with Conlon tomorrow."

"That makes two of us," Clint said.

THIRTY-THREE

Clint went back to his hotel and found that Alicia had not waited for him. It was just as well. He undressed and went to bed.

The next morning, he joined Bat for breakfast in the hotel dining room and told him about the events of the night before.

"I must be gettin' old if I slept through that," Bat complained.

"I think if I'd been asleep, I might not have heard it myself," Clint said.

"What were you doin' instead of sleepin'?"

Clint hesitated, then said, "Reading."

"Uh-huh."

Clint explained about the undertaker, and about Trench and his men, how the sheriff knew nothing about this apparent security force that Conlon had.

"I'm amazed we've only had two shooting incidents in the past two days," Bat said.

"Five dead men," Clint said. "That's plenty for me."

"So what do you want to do today?" Bat asked. "Time to get out of town?"

"You can leave if you want," Clint said. "I came here for a wake, and I'm going to get one."

"That means talking to Conlon."

"Burle's going to talk to him today," Clint said, "and so am I."

"Well," Bat said, "I'll come along to see that."

"Aren't you still afraid you'll want to shoot him?" Clint asked.

"Well, sure," Bat said, "but you won't let me."

"I just may stop you," Clint said, "by shooting him myself."

Bat laughed and said, "Now that I'd pay to see!"

They continued their breakfast and the conversation turned to Craddock.

"Is he even still around?" Bat asked.

"I haven't seen him leave," Clint said, "but then I haven't seen him since he went upstairs with one of the girls."

"Well, add him into the mix with all of us—plus this fella Trench—and I don't think we've seen nothin' yet."

"That's what I'm afraid of."

Clint's first stop was the sheriff's office.

"Just wanted to check and see if you talked to Conlon yet about last night."

"Not yet," Burle said. "Why?"

"We're going over there to talk to him about the wake," Clint said. "We want to get some answers about why it hasn't happened yet. And why he lied about the reasons."

"Knowing Conlon," Burle said, "he just sees a way to make money."

"You do know him well, then," Bat said.

"Well enough. All right," Burle said. "I'll hold off so I don't interrupt you."

"Good enough," Clint said.

"Let me know what happens."

"Will do."

Clint and Bat left the office.

* * *

They found the front doors of the Crystal open as they approached.

"I thought we'd have to bang on the doors to get in," Bat said.

"He might be trying to make up for the business he lost last night when he had to close."

They stepped up onto the boardwalk and entered through the batwing doors. The bartender—working on the bar with a damp rag—looked up at them.

"Mornin', gents," he said. "What'll it be?"

"Your boss," Clint said.

"Mr. Conlon is up in his office."

"Is he awake?"

"I think so," the man said. "I saw him earlier this mornin' when I got here. Boy, was he mad about havin' to close last night,"

"But not upset that his men had to kill three other men, huh?" Clint asked.

The bartender shrugged. "I dunno about that. We didn't talk about it."

"Well, we'll just go up and see how upset he is," Clint said.

The bartender knew who they both were, so he offered neither advice nor resistance.

THIRTY-FOUR

Clint and Bat went up the stairs and knocked on Conlon's office door. The man opened the door, dressed in his rumpled black suit.

"Well, well," Conlon said, "to what do I owe this visit so early?"

Clint poked Conlon in the chest, driving him back a few steps, then stepped inside, followed by Bat.

"You've been lying," Clint said.

"You'll have to be more specific," Conlon said. "I lie about a lot of things."

"This so-called wake," Clint said. "I talked to Driscoll, the undertaker. He says he doesn't know anything about it. He's not holding things up."

"Why would he?" Conlon asked.

"You said you couldn't show the body until you got the okay from the undertaker."

"I said that?"

"You did."

Conlon frowned.

"That's funny," he said. "I could've sworn I said the doctor."

"You said undertaker."

"I thought I said doctor," Conlon said again. "In fact, that's what I meant."

"Or is that just another lie?"

Conlon shrugged.

"All I know is I can't display the body . . . yet. Especially not after last night."

"That's something else," Clint said. "How long has Trench worked for you?"

"Why is that your business?"

"Because he killed three men last night," Clint said, "and in case you haven't noticed, I'm wearing a badge."

"I did notice," Conlon said. "Congratulations. Will you be settling here in Santa Fe?"

"No, this is temporary."

"Too bad," Conlon said. "You wearing a badge, too, Bat?"

Bat opened his jacket to show that he was not wearing a badge.

"You still haven't answered my question, Conlon," Clint said.

"I still don't think it's any of your business, but I'll answer you anyway," Conlon said. "Trench has been working for me for a couple of months. He's in charge of security for my saloon."

"What does that mean?"

"Just what it sounds like," Conlon said. "Just what he did last night."

"Well, you'll have to explain to the sheriff about last night," Clint said.

"That's fine," Conlon said. "I expect to have to defend the actions of my men, and I'll do so. Can I do anything else for you?"

"Yes," Clint said, "you better get the wake under way unless you want more incidents like last night."

"Is that an order?"

"It's a suggestion," Clint said. "You can take it or leave it."

"I'll give it some thought, Adams," Conlon said. "Is that all?"

"That's all," Clint said, "for now."

"You can see yourselves out," Conlon said. "Nice to see you, Bat."

Bat didn't say a word as he and Clint went to the door and left.

Outside the door, Bat looked at Clint and said, "You should've shot him."

"I was thinking the same thing," Clint said. He walked to the railing and looked down. A few customers had straggled in and were standing at the bar. Bat moved up alongside him and also looked down.

"He's playing with us all, and we're letting him."

"All the more reason to give it up and just leave town," Bat said.

"I'm tempted," Clint said, "but I can't walk out on Burle so soon after he gave me this badge. He's relying on Bass and me to back his play."

"I understand that," Bat said.

"You can go, though."

"Nah," Bat said. "I'll stick around as long as you and Luke are here. Maybe I can keep you boys out of trouble."

"Come on," Clint said, "I'll buy you a beer."

"A little early, isn't it?"

"Let's just call it an extension of breakfast," Clint suggested.

"I can live with that," Bat said.

THIRTY-FIVE

Clint and Bat took up a place at the end of the bar and ordered two beers. They were halfway through them when the sheriff walked in. He joined them at the bar. The place still had only a few customers.

"Beer?" Clint asked.

"Too early for me," Burle said. "Did you talk to Conlon?"

"We did," Clint said. "It wasn't a very satisfying conversation."

"Well, I better go up and talk to him myself, then."

"Hey," Clint said, "have you seen Thad today? What happened to him last night?"

"Thad is a heavy sleeper," Burle said. "He's over at the office now."

As Burle walked to the stairs and started up, Bat Masterson looked at Clint and said, "I can understand that."

They heard Burle knock on Conlon's door, heard it open, and after a few muttered words, they assumed he went inside.

"I don't think he's going to get much satisfaction either," Clint said.

"I should've shot Conlon five years ago when I caught him cheating," Bat said.

"Is that your beef with him?"

"I hate cheaters," Bat said.

"Why didn't you shoot him?"

"Because five years ago is when I started getting more civilized."

"Well, some people would say civilization isn't all it's cracked up to be."

"Amen," Bat said.

It only took fifteen minutes for Sheriff Burle to come back down. By that time Heck Thomas had joined Clint and Bat at the bar, and the place had started to fill up as people realized it was already open.

Clint, Bat, and Heck all turned to face the lawman, a beer in each of their left hands.

"How'd it go?"

"It's frustrating," Burle said. "I warned him that his security force better not kill anyone else, but he does have the right to protect his property."

"Ready for that beer now?" Clint asked.

"Hell, yes!" Burle said.

Craddock woke up and glanced at the naked girl next to him. He looked out the window and judged that he had slept too long. Well, but too long.

He got up and walked to the window. There were already people on the street, having already started their day.

He rubbed his hands over his face. He was getting old. He'd be forty on his next birthday, and he hadn't slept this late in years. Not even after a night of sex with a whore.

But they had quit early last night, he recalled, and gone to sleep.

He walked to the bed, where the naked girl had somehow hiked her butt up in the air while still asleep. She was pretty, and his penis began to harden as he looked at her butt. However, he couldn't afford to spend any more time with her.

He walked to the dresser against the wall, used the pitcher and basin to wash his face, neck, chest, and pits. As an afterthought he soaked a cloth and washed his crotch. Then he got dressed and strapped his gun on.

He walked to the bed, looked down at the whore again, then slapped her soundly on her raised butt.

"Ow!" she howled, turning over. "Wha—"

"I don't know what time you have to go to work, but I thought you'd like to know it's late."

"Wha—" she said again, looking around.

"Last night was great," he said. He took out some money and put it on the stand next to the bed. "There ya go. Enough?"

She didn't bother to look, just waved at him and said, "Yeah, yeah, it's fine." She fell back on the bed and sprawled out, her arms wide. He stared at her taut breasts, the dark nipples, felt a stirring, and abruptly went to the door and left.

Burle left after one beer, while Clint, Bat, and Heck Thomas ordered a second one each. The saloon continued to fill up and the talk they overheard led them to believe that most of the people there expected the wake to take place that day.

When Craddock came down the stairs, Clint saw him right away, nudged his two colleagues.

"Well, okay," Bat said, "Craddock's still in town."

The bounty hunter went to the bar and ordered a beer. But this time John Wesley Hardin had already claimed his former place at the bar. The batwings opened and Jim Miller walked in. Clay Allison had not yet arrived.

But the gang was almost all there!

THIRTY-SIX

In the next half hour Clint and Bass Reeves broke up two fights that threatened gunplay. Reeves had come in about five minutes before the first fight.

Two cowhands got into it over a saloon girl and almost went for their guns. Clint and Reeves didn't make them change their minds, just their location.

"You wanna kill each other?" Reeves asked.

"Do it outside," Clint said, and they tossed both men out the door.

Next, two cowboys started a fight over two bits somebody had left on the bar. Clint and Reeves threw them and the two bits out into the street.

Later, Bat Masterson said, "I've had more beer these last few days than I've ever had before."

"I know what you mean," Clint said, swirling what was left at the bottom of his mug.

Luke Short, who had joined them just a few minutes before, said, "Maybe we should just rush that room and get it over with."

"We'd have to go against Trench and his guards," Heck Thomas said.

"Do you think they could stand against us?" Luke asked. "What if we enlisted the aid of Hardin, Allison, and Miller? What then?"

"A bloodbath," Clint said. "Granted, we'd come out on top, but it would leave too many men dead."

"And Clint and I wouldn't be able to go along with the act," Bass Reeves said. "Not while we wear these deputy's badges."

"So then what? We continue to wait?" Luke asked.

"Any one of us can leave at any time," Clint said. "If your only goal here is to make sure he's dead, we can certainly pass the word on that."

"Well, speaking for myself," Heck said, "I'd still like to see it with my own eyes."

"This doesn't make any sense," Luke said. "Keepin' us waitin' this way."

"Agreed," Bat said, "but what can we do? Drag Conlon down from his office and force him to bring the body out?"

"Bloodshed again," Clint said.

"Yeah . . ." Bat said.

Clint looked farther down the bar.

"I'm surprised those fellas are still here, waiting," he said.

"Hardin?" Heck said. "Allison and Miller? What's the rush for them? None of them are wanted here."

"And then there's Craddock," Reeves said. "He's still around, isn't he?"

"Yes," Clint said. "We saw him this morning. He came down from upstairs, had a drink, and left."

"Could he have left town?" Luke asked.

"I doubt it," Clint said. "As long as there's to be a wake, he'll wait and see if Tom Horn arrives."

"So we all wait," Bat said, "because of Conlon. And we drink his beer and whiskey and put money in his pockets."

"Well," Clint said, "why didn't we think of that before?"

"Think of what?" Reeves asked.

"Let's take our money somewhere else," Clint said. "We'll drink somewhere else. That'll take profit from his pocket."

"How so?" Reeves asked. "The five of us drinkin' elsewhere will do that?"

"Five men with reputations," Clint said. "Don't you think others will follow us? Wanting to drink where Bat Masterson drinks? And Heck Thomas?"

"And the Gunsmith," Luke said.

"Yes."

"Well, okay, then," Heck said. "Where to, boys?"

"I know just the place," Clint said.

THIRTY-SEVEN

"Well, well," the bartender, Kelly O'Day, said as they walked into the Buckskin, "is the wake over?"

"Hasn't even started," Clint said.

"Then what brings you and your friends here?" O'Day asked.

"We decided to stop putting money into Ben Conlon's pockets," Bat said, "and do our waiting somewhere else."

"Well," O'Day said, "I'm happy to have such distinguished gentlemen in my place. First round is on the house, gents."

He set five beers up for the five men. The few others in the small saloon stayed away from the five men with deadly reputations, but they did not leave the place. They still wanted to drink there, just not next to the famous lawmen and gunmen.

And little by little, as the day went on, more men came into the Buckskin, having left the Crystal in search of the five famous men.

The plan was working. The Buckskin was filled to the rafters, and the Crystal Queen was losing money it otherwise would have had.

* * *

Ben Conlon looked down at the saloon floor and frowned. He expected to see more people. And when he looked at the bar, his frown deepened.

"They're gone," Alicia said, coming up alongside him.

"Who?"

"You know who," she said. "Clint Adams, Bat Masterson, and the others. The men you were counting on to keep bringing people into your saloon."

"Where'd they go?"

"Somewhere else," she said. "What does it matter? They're not here anymore. And others are following them."

"We still have those three," Conlon said, indicating Hardin, Miller, and Clay Allison.

"And the young lawman, Baca," she said, "but it's not enough."

Conlon could see that.

"It might be time, Ben," she said.

"Time for what?"

"You know," she said, "the wake. Start the wake."

He looked at her.

"What's wrong?" she asked.

"Nothing," he said. "Nothing's wrong."

The bartender looked up at his boss, and Conlon waved to him.

"Go back to your room, Alicia, and mind your own business," Conlon said.

He turned and went into his office.

Instead of going to her room, Alicia waited while the bartender came up.

"What's goin' on?" he asked.

"That's what I want to know," she said. "What do you know about the body?"

The man shrugged. "Nothin'. I ain't even ever seen it."

She nodded. He stepped to the door and knocked. When Conlon said, "Come!" he entered.

Alicia went to her room, but not to stay there. She got her wrap, and left again. She went down the back stairs, and out the back way.

The bartender entered his boss's office and didn't have to say a word.

"Get me Trench!" Conlon growled.

"Yessir!"

Clint was surprised when he saw Alicia walk into the Buckskin.

"Well, well," Bat said. "What do you think she wants?"

"Maybe," Clint said, "she wants us back."

Alicia looked around the small saloon, spotted Clint, and walked over.

"Can we talk?" she asked.

"Sure," he said, "go ahead."

She looked around at his friends and said, "Alone?"

Although the Buckskin was busier than it had ever been, there were still tables available. Clint walked Alicia to one in the back and they sat down.

"You made the right move, you know," she said.

"Did I?"

"You and all your friends," she said. "You're hurting Conlon where it matters to him, in his wallet."

"It's his own fault," Clint said. "A bunch of us are also on the verge of leaving town, figuring the wake is just a big hoax."

She did not reply.

"Is it?"

"I honestly don't know."

"You haven't seen the body?"

"Even if I did, I wouldn't recognize it."

"But you have seen a body, right?"

She hesitated, then said, "No—but I don't want to see any dead bodies."

"So you don't know what Conlon's up to."

"He's up to what he's always up to," she said, "makin' money."

"Well, if he doesn't start that wake soon, he may not have a place," Clint said.

"What have you heard?"

"People are becoming impatient," Clint said. "Evidenced by those three last night. There'll be more bloodshed, and that's if somebody doesn't just burn the place down."

Her eyes widened.

"Have you heard someone threaten that?"

"Right now people are just talking," Clint said, since he'd never really heard anyone suggest that. He was just trying to scare her and, in turn, maybe Conlon.

"Tell your boss he better get it started before he loses more customers."

She frowned and said, "I will."

He walked her to the front door under the eyes of most of the customers, who recognized her from the Crystal.

"Come and see me later," she said, touching his arm.

"If I can," he said.

She nodded and left. Clint rejoined his friends at the bar again.

"What was that about?" Luke asked.

"Or was it personal?" Bat added.

"Not personal," Clint said, and told them about the conversation.

"That was good thinking," Heck said, "mentioning somebody burning the place down."

"Yeah," Reeves said, "maybe somethin' will get done now."

"I hope so," Bat said. "I don't know if I can drink another beer."

THIRTY-EIGHT

Craddock was sitting in front of the hotel when the man rode in on a roan pony. Craddock narrowed his eyes as he tried to see the man's face beneath the pulled-down brim of his hat.

He wasn't sure, but he thought the man was Tom Horn.

As the rider passed him—paying him no apparent mind—he stood up so he could watch him ride all the way down the street. As he watched, the man reined in his horse in front of the Crystal Queen, dismounted, and went inside.

Craddock started walking toward the saloon, still watching the man.

As the man entered the saloon, he looked around, saw two men he knew, but ignored them. He walked to the bar and ordered a beer.

Farther down the bar, John Wesley Hardin saw the man enter and thought he recognized him. He looked over at Miller and Clay Allison, wondering if they did, too.

Miller nudged Allison and said, "Is that Tom Horn?"

Allison turned his head to have a look.

"I think so."

"First Craddock, now Horn," Miller said. "I wonder who they're after."

"With any luck," Allison said, turning back to his beer, "each other."

Craddock stopped in front of the batwing doors and looked in. He saw the man standing at the bar, but could only see his back. He still didn't know for sure if this was Horn or not.

He came through the batwings, figuring there was only one way to find out.

Trench entered Conlon's office and stood in front of his desk with his hands clasped in front of him.

"You wanted to see me?"

"I want you to double the guard on that room," Conlon said.

"Okay."

"But I want you to do something else."

"What?"

"Sit down," Conlon said, "and I'll explain . . ."

Elfego Baca watched from his table as the stranger entered and walked to the bar, then saw Craddock appear at the door and walk in. He also wondered where Clint Adams and the other lawmen and ex-lawmen had gone.

A man came running into the Buckskin and shouted, "We think Craddock has found his man in the Crystal."

Clint and Bat exchanged a quick glance.

"Horn?" Bat asked.

"We better go and see."

"What if it's a trick to get us back to the Crystal?" Luke asked.

"Then I'd say it worked."

Clint and Bat left the Buckskin, while Heck Thomas and Luke Short stayed behind.

                      *   *   *

Craddock took up a position at the bar, about halfway
between John Wesley Hardin and the stranger he thought
might be Tom Horn. By using the mirror behind the bar, he
determined that he was right. It was Horn.

"Beer?" the bartender asked.

"Whiskey," Craddock said. He always had whiskey
before he was going to kill a man.

Trench came out of Conlon's office, looked down at the
saloon floor, then went back to the office.

"Hey, boss," he said, "I think you better come out and
watch this."

Conlon came out of his office.

"What is it?"

Trench pointed down and said, "Craddock. I think he
found his man."

"How can you tell?"

"He ordered whiskey," Trench said. "Craddock always
orders whiskey before he kills."

Conlon stared down with interest.

THIRTY-NINE

As Clint and Bat entered the saloon, they could feel the tension in the air. Everyone's attention seemed to be on the bar. They looked that way and Clint recognized Craddock.

Elfego Baca came up alongside Clint and said in a whisper, "He is drinking whiskey."

"Oh," Clint said.

"What does that mean?" Bat asked.

Clint looked at his friend. "He always drinks whiskey before he kills somebody."

"Really? That's what he's known for?"

Clint nodded. Baca went back to his seat and looked on with interest.

"You're wearing a badge," Bat said. "That means you can't just stand by and watch."

"I know."

Clint studied the backs of the men at the bar, stopped when he saw one in particular.

"Is that Tom Horn?" Clint asked.

"I don't know him from the back," Bat said, "but it could be."

"Bat," Clint said, "cover me from here. We don't know who'll take Craddock's side."

"Gotcha."

Clint walked toward the bar, and the man he thought might be Tom Horn. Several men moved away to give him room.

He stood alongside the man, who appeared to be engrossed in his beer.

"Hello, Tom."

"Adams," Horn said without turning his head. His trail clothes were covered with dust. He'd been on the trail a long time.

"What brings you here?" Clint asked.

"Same as you, I suspect," Horn said. "A wake. Did I miss it?"

"It hasn't started yet."

"Good. I want to see for myself if the bastard is dead." Horn looked at him. "Buy you a beer?"

"Craddock is here."

"Craddock? The bounty hunter?" Horn asked. "Why should that interest me?"

"He says he's after you," Clint said. "He's got paper on you from Arizona."

Horn frowned.

"The Pleasant Valley thing?" he said.

"That's my guess."

"I didn't do anythin' wrong there."

"I don't think he cares."

"Where is he?"

"About fifteen feet to our right."

"What's he doin'?"

"Drinking whiskey."

"Hmm."

"Horn!" Craddock snapped.

The men at the bar between them quickly darted away. Craddock turned to face Horn, but Clint was still between them.

"Step aside, Adams," Craddock said.

"No."

"Do it, Clint," Horn said.

"No," Clint said. "You're not a gunfighter, Tom. He'll kill you."

"Probably."

"He may not be a gunfighter," Craddock said, "but he's a killer. I'm takin' him in."

"I'm the law here, Craddock," Clint said. "You're not killing him."

"I didn't say I was gonna kill him," Craddock said. "I'm takin' him in."

"We all know what it means when you take somebody in."

"So you're gonna stop me, Adams?" Craddock asked. "You're gonna fight me?"

"If I have to."

Craddock raised his voice.

"I'll share the bounty on Horn with any man who stands with me."

Nobody moved, or replied. Then suddenly, one man stepped forward.

"I'll take a piece of that," Clay Allison said.

"Me, too," Killin' Jim Miller said. They moved away from the bar and spread out. The saloon's patrons flattened themselves against the walls, but nobody tried to leave. This was the kind of thing they'd been waiting for.

"Count me in," a third man said. And then a fourth. Soon, Clint and Horn were facing eight men.

"I don't like these odds," Horn said.

Upstairs, Trench said to Conlon, "What do you want me to do?"

"You want to side with someone?" Conlon asked. "Who?"

Alicia appeared at the rail and asked, "What's happening?"

"Watch," Conlon said. "This is gonna make us famous."

FORTY

Clint watched Craddock. He was the key. The action was his to call. Allison and Miller, and the others, wouldn't move until he did.

But the fact remained it was two against eight, until . . .

Bat Masterson moved up alongside Clint and said, "The odds just got better."

Three against eight.

"We've got them right where we want them," Clint said.

"*Perdón, amigos,*" Elfego Baca said, "but two-to-one is much better odds, don't you think?"

Better, Clint thought, but Allison and Miller were fast guns. There was no way to know who was faster, them or Clint or Bat. Horn was not a gunfighter. Baca was good with a gun, but not a gunfighter.

Clint looked up and saw Conlon, Alicia, and Trench, who were watching the proceedings, then looked around at the others who were watching.

"Just hold on," Clint said.

"What for?" Craddock asked.

"Just look around," Clint said. "All of you. Look around. We're putting on a show for the rest of these idiots. And for them, up there." He pointed.

Craddock looked up, as did Allison and Miller.

"That's Conlon up there, in the middle. He owns this place. And we're about to make it famous. Some of us are going to die here, and he's going to make money because of it."

Craddock looked back at Clint.

"You've got at least five or six of us here who know what we're doing with a gun," Clint said. "Who's faster, we don't know, but we're all deadly. Yet you've got some men on your side we know nothing about. That makes for stray bullets. Stray bullets make for dead innocent bystanders—innocent bystanders who are too stupid to leave because they want to see the show."

Craddock, Allison, and Miller stared at Clint. Behind them Clint could see John Wesley Hardin smiling. He obviously had a brain.

"I get it," Hardin said. "You all might as well be dancing monkeys."

Clint could see the men he was facing thinking about that. He assumed that the men on either side of him were also thinking about it.

Finally, Clay Allison spoke. "I ain't nobody's monkey." He spread his hands and stepped back, took up a position next to Hardin, who handed him a beer.

"What do you suggest?" Craddock asked.

"Everybody just step back," Clint said. "This doesn't have to happen today. Not in here anyway."

He could see Craddock considering his words.

He raised his voice.

"We're all here for a wake," Clint said. "Why kill each other while we're waiting? And why wait any longer?"

The batwings opened at that point and Sheriff Burle walked in, flanked by Bass Reeves, Thad, and Billy. They were all carrying rifles.

"Nobody's killing anybody today!" Burle called out. "Not in my town."

After a moment of silence Craddock said, "Relax, Sheriff. It's all just been a misunderstanding." He turned to the bar and picked up his beer. A collective sigh was heaved by the customers—for half of them it was relief, and the other half disappointment.

Craddock's supporters backed off. Miller went back to his beer. The other, lesser known men who had tried to get involved went back to their tables. Men peeled themselves off the walls and went back to their tables and drinks.

Horn looked at Clint, Bat, and Elfego Baca and said, "Appreciate the support, gents."

"De nada, amigo," Baca said, and went back to his table.

Sherriff Burle came over to them, leaving his deputies at the door—except for Reeves.

"Tom," Reeves said.

"Hello, Bass."

Reeves looked around.

"Where's Heck? He missed the action."

"Luke, too," Bat said.

"Luckily," Clint said, "there didn't turn out to be much action." He looked up at Conlon, who was still watching. "Much to the disappointment of Mr. Conlon."

"What was this about?" Burle asked.

Apparently, he'd not connected Reeves's "Hello, Tom" to Tom Horn yet.

"Just another tense moment," Clint said. "The wake is way overdue."

"I agree," Burle said. "Let's see what I can do about that."

"You going to talk to Conlon again?" Clint asked.

"I am."

"Want company?"

"Naw," Burle said, "you and Bass stay here, keep my two young deputies out of trouble."

FORTY-ONE

Burle entered Conlon's office and closed the door, leaving Trench and Alicia outside.

"Things don't seem to be going so well," Burle said, sitting down.

Conlon got up, poured two glasses of brandy, and handed one to Burle. Then he sat behind his desk again.

"It almost did," Conlon said. "You came in a little too late."

"In time to hear Adams talk them all out of it," Burle pointed out. "Not the dancing monkeys we were hoping for."

"Without him, it would have worked," Conlon said. "They would've started shooting. Somebody would have died. We could have owned the place where Bat Masterson died, or where Clay Allison bought it, for where Heck Thomas caught a bullet."

"Along with a lot of innocent bystanders," Burle said.

Conlon waved that off.

"Small cost to build a big reputation," he said.

Burle sipped his drink.

"We'll have to send Trench after Adams," Burle said. "Get him out of the way. It's the only answer."

"What about the wake?" Conlon asked. "It's got to start sometime."

"You forget," Burle said, leaning forward. "We don't really have a body. How can we start a wake?"

"You know," Conlon said, "when you came up with this harebrained scheme, it sounded good to me."

"And now?"

"Now I'm not so sure."

"Don't worry about it," Burle said. "Just let me do the thinkin', Ben, and things will turn out all right. Now get Trench in here. I want to talk to him."

"I already talked with him——"

"What did I just say about thinkin'?" Burle asked.

Conlon shut his mouth, frowned, then stood up and walked to the door. "Trench," he said.

The security man entered the office. Alicia, still standing at the rail, craned her neck to get a look into the room. Conlon smiled at her and closed the door.

"Give the man a drink, Ben," Burle said. "We're gonna talk."

"And what are you gonna tell them downstairs? I mean, why you were in here so long?"

"Don't worry so much, Ben," Burle said. "Just get Captain Trench a drink—a real drink."

The two young deputies took up position at the near end of the bar, close to the front window, and nursed a beer each.

Clint studied the two young deputies, then looked up toward Conlon's office, where Burle had gone.

"Bass."

"Yeah?"

Clint pointed. "Why would you hire those two as deputies?"

"I wouldn't," Reeves said. "They're okay kids, but they'll never make good lawmen. What's your point?"

"That is my point," Clint said. "Why would Burle hire them as deputies?"

"He said he couldn't get anybody else," Reeves pointed out.

"In a town this size?" Clint asked. "Wouldn't you think he'd have his pick?"

"I would think that, but . . . are you sayin' what I think you're sayin'?"

Clint asked, "What do you think I'm saying?"

"That he purposely hired two young men he knows can't do the job?"

"Okay," Clint said, "that's what I'm saying."

"But why?"

"Now that's a question I'd really like the answer to."

FORTY-TWO

Clint and Reeves went over to the Buckskin with Bat, Luke, and Heck. Tom Horn decided to go along with them, instead of staying in the Crystal with Craddock.

Craddock, seeing Horn walk out with Clint and Bass Reeves, decided to let him go. No sense bracing him in the street with those two along. Besides, he didn't think Horn would leave town. That would look too much like running.

"Craddock?"

The bounty hunter turned, looked at Killin' Jim Miller.

"Yeah?"

"You still offerin' that money for Horn?"

"You help me take him down, I'll pass some of that bounty money on to you."

"As long as it don't mean tanglin' with the Gunsmith," Miller said, "you got a deal."

"What about Allison?"

"You'll have to talk to him about that."

Craddock looked down the bar, decided that before he talked to Clay Allison, he'd take a run at John Wesley Hardin. Of the three, he figured Hardin had the fastest gun, might have the best chance of taking the Gunsmith out of the play.

"I'll let you know," he told Miller.

"Good enough," Miller said, and went back to his beer.

"You're sayin' what?" Heck Thomas asked.

"There's no body," Clint said. "That's why Conlon's holding up the wake."

"Then what was the point?" Reeves asked.

"Getting men like us into town with men like Hardin, Allison, Miller, Craddock, and seeing what happens."

"Like what almost happened in the Crystal."

"That place would not just have been famous," Clint said, "it would have been infamous."

"But what if a showdown like that didn't happen in his place?" Luke Short asked.

"Then it would happen in town," Clint said. "He still benefits when Santa Fe becomes known as the place where Bat Masterson was killed."

"Or the Gunsmith," Bat said.

"Right."

"So what do we do?" Heck asked.

"We get a look at that body."

"Which means goin' against Trench and his men," Luke Short said.

"Right," Clint said.

"So we get the sheriff to go in with us," Reeves suggested.

"I've got some thoughts about him, too," Clint said. "Goes back to what I said about him hiring inept deputies."

"We're listening," Bat said.

"Is this really what you want?" Alicia asked Conlon in his office. "A gunfight in front of your place?" She had entered while Conlon was still talking with Sheriff Burle. The lawman had stood up, doffed his hat to her, and left.

"This is exactly what I want," he said. "Do you know the names of the men who will get killed here? They're legendary!"

"If they are legendary, how did you get Trench and his men to go against them?"

"Money," Conlon said, "and ego. With Trench's men, it's money, but with him, it's ego. See, he wants to be a legend, and he can achieve that by killing himself some legends."

"And what about you?" she asked. "What do you want to be? The man who put on a phony wake?"

"I want to be rich, Alicia," Conlon said. "That's what this is all about. Inside my place, in front of my place, it's all the same to me. As long as the Gunsmith or Bat Masterson falls, I make money."

"You're a sick man, Ben."

"Maybe," Conlon said, "but I'll be a rich sick man."

Trench collected his best men, moved out onto the boardwalk in front of the saloon with them. He had four other men still in the room with the casket, but he didn't think they'd be pressed into service.

"What's goin' on, Trench?"

He turned his head, looked at Craddock, standing just outside the batwing doors. They knew each other, but had not spoken until now.

"What's it to you, Craddock?"

"Well," the bounty hunter said, "if you're settin' up to do what I think you're doin', I just might join you."

"Why would you do that?"

"Because I got a price to collect on Tom Horn's head and I don't want anybody else getting it."

"I don't care about no bounty money," Trench said. "You can have it. But what makes you think Horn will come along with the others?"

Craddock shrugged and asked, "Why not?"

"You bringin' anybody with you?"

"Jim Miller."

"I wouldn't say no to havin' him on my side," Trench told him.

Craddock looked at the ten men Trench had with him in front of the Crystal.

"You think you got enough men?"

"I do now," Trench said.

"We're talkin' about Clint Adams, Bat Masterson, Bass Reeves, Heck Thomas, Luke Short, and maybe Tom Horn," Craddock said. "There ain't a slouch in there."

"We got 'em outnumbered."

"Might also be Elfego Baca."

"Don't matter," Trench said, "My men are battle tested and hard, and with you and Miller along, we got thirteen."

"You gonna have any trouble with the law?"

"The law is in Conlon's pocket," Trench said, "or the other way around. Either way, he ain't gonna be a concern."

"You got this all figured, huh?"

"Pretty much," Trench said. "I was you, I'd go and get Miller so he don't miss none of the action."

"I'll do it."

"See if you can get John Wesley Hardin and Clay Allison, too," Trench said. "That'd pretty much give us an unbeatable edge."

FORTY-THREE

"So you're calling for us to all go over there and brace Trench and his men," Heck Thomas said.

"I am."

"What if they don't back down?" Reeves said.

"Look who we have here," Clint said, pointing up and down the Buckskin bar, where they were standing. "Who would go up against this?"

"An egomaniac," Bat said.

"A what?" Reeves asked.

"A man looking for a reputation," Luke Short said.

"Not to mention money," Tom Horn said.

"Tom's right," Heck said. "Trench's men are probably gettin' paid plenty to face us."

The bartender, O'Day, spoke up after listening awhile.

"You want I should send somebody over to take a look at the Crystal?" he asked.

"That's a good idea, Kelly," Clint said. "Let's get some idea of what Conlon and Trench are planning."

"You got it."

O'Day went to the end of the bar and talked to a man, who then ran out through the batwings, leaving them swinging behind him.

"He'll be right back," he told them.

"So what do we have?" Clint asked. "Five of us?"

"Six," Horn said. "I'm in."

"Why?" Clint asked. "This isn't your fight, Tom. You just got here."

"You stood with me against Craddock," Horn said. "That's all the reason I need."

"What about Baca?" Reeves asked. "He's still in the Crystal."

"That'll be up to him," Clint said. "Let's just say there's six of us for now."

"This is all so stupid," Bat said. "We all got sucked in by Conlon. All of us, along with the likes of Hardin, Allison, and Miller. We should all just ride out, leave Conlon with an empty saloon."

"We could do that," Clint said. "Why don't we put it to a vote? I'll go along with the majority."

"Why don't we wait for O'Day's man to come back before we decide?" Luke said.

At that moment the man came bursting through the doors, pointing behind him.

"They got a bunch of men waitin' in front of the Crystal," he said.

"Who?"

"I dunno all of 'em," the man said. "Trench is leadin' 'em, and they got that bounty hunter and Killin' Jim Miller standin' with them."

"Not Hardin?" Heck Thomas asked. "Or Allison?"

"Not that I saw. Just a bunch of Trench's security guards—or whatever he calls 'em."

"Thanks, Pete," O'Day said. "Have a drink on the house."

"Thanks, Kelly."

Pete went to the other end of the bar.

"Looks like we may have had the vote taken out of our hands," Luke said.

"How so?" Bat asked.

"You think they're going to let us walk past the saloon to the livery to get our horses?"

"They want this to happen," Heck said.

"Which means," Bat added, "they think they've got an edge."

"Well," Clint said, "they've got the law on their side, if we're right."

"And maybe more guns than you can see out front," Tom Horn said.

"That means the rooftops," Bat said, "and maybe some windows."

"How do we manage to switch the edge over to us?" Luke Short asked.

"I think for that," Clint said, "we probably just have to show up."

FORTY-FOUR

Clint, Bat, Luke, Heck Thomas, Bass Reeves, and Tom Horn all left the Buckskin and started walking over to the Crystal.

"You know," Bat said to Clint as they brought up the rear, "if they don't back off, we'll have to go through with this."

"I know it," Clint said, "but I'm tired of waiting, and I'm tired of being played."

"Well," Bat said, "I'd sure like it better if Conlon was on the street with his men."

"We can go and see him after," Clint said.

"If there is an after," Bat said. "You know there's a chance one of us will catch a lucky bullet."

"There's always that chance," Clint said.

Bat looked up and down the street as they came within sight of the Crystal.

"What are you looking for?" Clint asked.

"The sheriff," Bat said. "I thought maybe he'd put in an appearance on this."

"He will," Clint said, "when the shooting is all over and done with."

"Here they come," Trench said. "Get ready."

"Is Horn with 'em?" Craddock asked.

"He's there," Trench said. He looked to his left at Sykes, his right hand. "Those men on the roof?"

"They're there, boss," Sykes said. "Across the street, and right above us."

"Good. This should go just fine."

Sheriff Burle watched from his position across the street as Clint, Bat, and the others approached the Crystal. If this worked out the way it was supposed to, he wouldn't have to wear his badge for very much longer. No more forty-a-month job for him.

Ever again.

As they approached the Crystal, they moved six abreast. Clint had Bat and Luke on his left, with Reeves, Heck, and Tom Horn on his right.

Trench knew what he was doing, as he had his men all fanned out in front of the saloon, including Dutch Craddock and Jim Miller. Clint was pleased to see that John Wesley Hardin and Clay Allison had decided not to take a hand in this game.

"Adams," Trench said.

"Trench," Clint said. "What's this about? We were just coming in for a drink."

"You and your friends already had lots of drinks in here," Trench said. "I think you're here for another reason."

"Same reason as always," Clint said. "A wake. We think it's time your boss got it under way."

"I think that's up to my boss."

"Well," Clint said, "we aim to help him make up his mind."

"You ain't comin' in, Adams."

"How do you intend to stop us, Trench?"

"The same way we stopped those others," Trench said. "We'll leave you all lyin' in the street, Mr. Gunsmith."

"No doubt there are going to be a lot of bodies lying in the street, Mr. Trench."

"Then call it," Trench said.

"I'm going to leave that to you, Trench," Clint said. "This bloodbath is going to be your mistake."

But even as he said it, he wasn't sure he was right. They had all had their chance to ride out and avoid bloodshed, but here they were. Sometimes a man just couldn't avoid making a mistake.

FORTY-FIVE

Alicia's room was in the front of the Crystal, so she was able to look down at the street. She could see Clint and his friends fanned out in front of the saloon. She could not see Trench and his men, but she knew they were on the boardwalk beneath her. But she *was* able to see the men with rifles that Trench had placed on the roof across the street. And if they were on that roof, they had to be on the roof above her as well. Clint and his friends were sitting ducks.

"Oh my God," she said, and ran downstairs.

Trench's men all looked to him for their cue. They were all assured of extra money if they came out of this alive. And it was enough money to make it well worth the risk that was involved with facing a bunch of Old West legends.

Craddock had his eyes on Tom Horn, who was looking right back at him. They only had eyes for each other, leaving the other men to deal with one another.

This was where Craddock expected to collect the considerable bounty he'd come for.

* * *

Killin' Jim Miller was simply in the mood to kill someone—anyone.

Why else would they call him Killin' Jim?

Clint was prepared for Trench to call the play, and the way he'd call it was to go for his gun. He was probably no fast draw, but a steady hand with a gun. A man who didn't panic, and could shoot, was much more dangerous than a fast gun. Fast guns often missed their first shot. A man with a steady hand did not miss.

Craddock was the same. He'd make his move smoothly and assured, not particularly fast. Clint decided to leave the bounty hunter to Horn.

But this surely wasn't all they would have to deal with. It couldn't be. His back was just itching way, way too much, and that was always bad news.

Trench took his time. He knew he was facing men of ability, men of experience, men who had killed before, but he still felt they had to be straining to pull their guns. And they were waiting for him.

Let them wait . . .

What the hell was holding everything up? Sheriff Burle wondered.

In his office Ben Conlon was waiting for the sound of shots.

Alicia was leading a man up the stairs to the second floor, and to the hatch that led to the roof.

Even the patrons of the saloon, who knew something was going on, were straining to hear.

Everybody was waiting for Trench.

Trench finally moved, and everything was set into motion . . .

FORTY-SIX

Clint was impressed.

Trench not only drew coolly and smoothly, but was pretty fast. Still, while Trench made the first move, the first shot was fired by the Gunsmith.

And then all hell broke loose . . .

Horn and Craddock drew together, and as Horn heard the first shot, he extended his gun toward the bounty hunter. They were both very deliberate, and fired at almost the same time . . .

The others knew that Clint was going to take Trench first, and Horn would handle Craddock. Bat and Luke drew their guns and simply began firing at the bodies in front of them.

Heck Thomas drew and immediately turned to fire at the rooftops behind them, as planned. If there had been no guns there, he would have turned back, but he quickly saw that the assumption they had all made had been correct. Trench had set up an ambush.

Bass Reeves drew and turned his attention to the rooftops above and in front of them. Surprised that there were no guns there, he quickly turned and assisted Heck Thomas with the guns that were behind them. Rifles fell from that roof, and men tumbled after them . . .

Clint's bullet struck Trench in the chest and drove him back through the batwing doors into the saloon, where he landed on his back, dead. The bartender left the bar and ran up to Conlon's office.

"Boss," he said, busting in, "Trench is dead!"

"Damn it!" Conlon said. He opened his top drawer, took out a gun, and set it on the desktop. "Get out!"

Craddock felt Horn's bullet as it punched into his shoulder. He fired, saw his bullet strike Horn in the side, but he knew it wasn't a killing shot. Neither was Horn's first, but his second hit Craddock in the chest, sent him crashing through the saloon window, where he joined Trench on the floor . . .

Killin' Jim Miller immediately saw that things were not going well. His horse was in front of the saloon, so he ran for it, mounted up, and rode out. No one cared that he was riding out, only that he wasn't shooting at them.

As Trench fell through the batwing doors, Clint turned his attention elsewhere. He also looked at the rooftops above them, but had no time to wonder why no one was shooting at them from there. He began firing at the uniformed security force, who seemed to be in a panic now that their boss was dead. Maybe they were wondering if they'd still get paid. But first they'd have to come through this alive.

As uniformed men fell in the street, the remaining force tossed their guns down and put their hands up.

It was over . . .

They checked the bodies to be sure they were dead. Clint looked around, expecting to see either Sheriff Burle or Ben Conlon, but neither man appeared.

"What happened up there?" Bat said, looking up at the rooftops. "Why put guns behind us, but not above us?"

"I don't know, but—"

At that moment the batwings opened and four men in uniforms came out, their hands in the air, with Elfego Baca behind them. He holstered his gun and smiled at Clint.

"These *pendejos* were on the roof. I think perhaps they were looking for trouble. I saved them."

"Much obliged, Elfego," Clint said.

"That was sure a big help," Heck Thomas said.

"*Por nada, mis amigos,*" Baca said. "I am happy to help. And am I to assume there will be no wake?"

"Probably not," Clint said, "but we were just going to go and check on that."

"*Bueno,*" the young lawman said. "I will remain out here and help."

Since the sheriff had not appeared, Bass Reeves—still wearing his deputy's badge—took control of the situation.

"Ready to go see Conlon?" Clint asked Bat.

"Yeah," Bat said. "But this time I think I'll shoot him."

FORTY-SEVEN

Clint and Bat marched into Conlon's office without knocking. From down the hall, Alicia came out and crept to the open doorway.

From behind his desk, Conlon looked up at them. His gun was still on the desk in front of him.

"Time for us to take a look at that body, Conlon," Bat said.

"Trench?"

"Dead," Clint said, "along with a bunch of his men."

"There are still some men in that room with the casket," Conlon said.

"Well, you're gonna tell them to open the door and put down their guns," Bat said.

"What for?"

"So we can see the body," Clint said.

"There's no need," Conlon said. "It's not him."

"So you have been lying," Clint said.

"Yes. But it wasn't my idea."

"Whose was it?" Clint asked.

"It was mine."

Clint and Bat turned, saw Sheriff Jim Burle holding Alicia in one hand and his gun in the other.

"You boys are under arrest," he said.

"For what?" Clint asked.

"For ruinin' my plans," Burle said. "But I'm gonna try to save them by putting you in my jail before you can talk and tell people what you know."

"What about the others?" Clint asked. "Bass Reeves, Heck Thomas, the rest. They'll talk."

"They'd only be guessing," Burle said. "You two are the only ones who know for sure."

"We'll tell them," Bat said, "even from jail."

"Not if you're killed tryin' to escape," Burle said with a smile.

"You know," Clint said, "I really underestimated you, Burle."

"Yeah, I know," Burle said. "That was part of the plan, too."

Burle was overconfident. He was standing with Alicia only partially shielding him.

"Well then, no," Clint said, "we won't be going to jail."

Burle waggled the barrel of his gun and said, "I think you are. Now drop those guns."

"I don't think so," Clint said. "Bat, you take Conlon. I'll take the sheriff."

"You'd shoot a man wearin' a badge, Adams?" Burle asked.

"You don't deserve to wear it."

"So what are you gonna do?" Burle asked. "Draw on me? With my gun already in my hand? And shoot me through this woman?"

"Bat?"

"Ready."

Too late Conlon grabbed for his gun. Bat drew and shot him through the chest.

Clint drew before Burle knew what was happening and shot the crooked lawman in the forehead. His eyes went wide, then he released both Alicia and his gun, and toppled over backward.

"Oh my God!" Alicia said, stunned. "You could have hit me!"

"Never," Bat assured her. "He only hits what he shoots at."

"Alicia," Clint said, "you better go down and get those men out of that room, tell them it's all over."

"What about the wake?" she asked.

"There's no wake, because there's no body," Clint said. "At least, not the body of Tanner Moody."

"Oh."

"And I think with Conlon dead," Clint said, "this place goes to you. What do you think?"

She grinned and said, "I think that's fine."

As she left, Bat said to Clint, "What are we going to tell those people downstairs?"

"That Tanner Moody is still alive out there somewhere," Clint said. "Those who really wanted him to be dead can go and look for him, and take care of it themselves."

Watch for

DEATH IN THE DESERT

383rd novel in the exciting GUNSMITH series
from Jove

Coming in November!

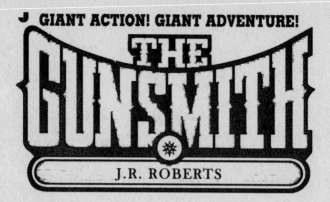